MCN LIBRARY
Marysville, WA 98270
AUG 2010

Whispering Stones

Whispering Stones

Sally Hawthorne

LANGMARC PUBLISHING • SAN ANTONIO, TEXAS

Whispering Stones

Sally Hawthorne

Editor: Renée Hermanson
Cover Artist: Aundrea Hernandez
Cover Graphics: Michael Qualben

Copyright © 1998 Sally Hawthorne
First Printing 1998
Printed in the United States of America

All rights reserved. No part of this book may be reproduced or transmitted in any form or by any means, electronic or mechanical, including photocopying, recording, or by any information storage and retrieval system, without the written permission from the publisher, except for review. Characters in this book are fictional and bear no resemblance to actual people.

Published by
LANGMARC PUBLISHING
P.O. 33817 • San Antonio, Texas 78265

Library of Congress Cataloging-in-Publication Data
Hawthorne, Sally.
    Whispering stones / Sally Hawthorne.
        p.   cm.
    ISBN 1-880292-60-2
   I. Title
PS3558.A8238W47   1998
  813'.54--dc21
                                          98-40562
                                              CIP

Dedication

For my sweet daughter
who has shared with me her
spiritual gift of encouragement.
I love you, Judi.

Acknowledgments

With appreciation to

Millie Barger, author of *Like Abigail,*
recently published by LangMarc;
Friends and family who made it possible for Jack and
me to spend a night in historic Ruthin Castle in Wales;
Donna Goodrich, author and speaker;
Ben Hanks, my son-in-law computer troubleshooter;
Editor Renée Hermanson;
Marshall Macaluso of Mission to the Americas,
who is also intrigued by castles;
Dr. Claude Moffitt, former General Director of the
Conservative Baptist Association of Arizona;
Susan Titus Osborn, editor of
The Christian Communicator;
Interior Designer Becky Peters, my grandson's wife;
Lois Qualben, my publisher at LangMarc;
My lawyer son, Stan, for his legal expertise;
Sally E. Stuart, author of *The Christian Writers' Guide;*
U.S. Immigration and Naturalization Service;
and last, but not least, Jack,
whose love and encouragement
—after sixty years—
has still spurred me on
from his bed in a nursing home.

My thanks to all of you.

Chapter One

Sari Wyatt's first impulse was to tear the telegram into tiny bits and toss it into the trash. "What kind of joke is this?" Sari asked herself angrily and brushed tears from her eyes when she heard her fiancé's special knock. She hurried to open the door.

"Hi, sweetheart," Michael Hancock greeted her. "I'm glad you're home early from work. I just had a great idea. How about taking our supper down to Central Park and—" His hazel eyes narrowed in sympathy. "What happened?"

Sari waved the telegram. "This is what happened. It's from a lawyer in Phoenix. For some reason, my grandmother has decided to contact me!"

"Isn't that good?"

"No! She has never bothered about me before and here she is, practically ordering me to come out to Arizona!"

"Arizona? That would sound pretty good to most anybody." He put his arms about her and added, "Sari darling, this is the first time you've mentioned a grandmother. I never knew she even existed."

"As far as I am concerned, she doesn't! And that was the way she wanted it." Frowning, Sari stepped out of his embrace. "The gist of the message is, she wants to see me on Friday. But, according to this, I'm welcome to arrive any day this week. So I need to make up my mind. Michael, would you mind leaving now?"

"Wouldn't it help to talk about it?"

"No! It would not." Sari took a deep breath. "I'm sorry. I don't mean to sound cross, but I am so upset."

"It's okay. However, we need to talk. I've noticed for quite awhile that something has been bothering you. Honey, I love you. I can't stand to see you so unhappy. Talk to me. Please."

"No!"

Michael had spoken the truth: something had been weighing heavily on Sari's mind. But this was not the time to talk.

With his expressive long-lashed hazel eyes, Michael looked like a lost puppy as she pushed him to the door and closed it behind him. Slumping against it, Sari realized for the first time that this unwelcome, unexpected summons from her grandmother was just what she needed right now.

It would put some space between Michael and herself; she could leave and avoid a painful scene with him. That was the only good thing about it.

The thought was still with her after a night of intermittent sleep, and she knew her decision had been made. Why wait? She would go to Arizona today.

Sari called her office, then caught a taxi that whisked her to Kennedy International Airport. Settled in her seat, she dozed most of the way. When she opened her eyes, she looked out the window to see what looked like an undulating sea of brown.

It seemed to stretch on to infinity. With her face against the window of the 747, Sari looked down at the vastness and willed herself not to cry.

She had not imagined that any other spot on earth could look so much like India's northern plains. She could almost see the swirling dust devils and feel the scorching heat. A flood of memories brought tears to Sari's eyes and she brushed at them, hoping no one would notice.

The motherly-looking woman seated next to her asked, "What is it, dear? Is there anything I can do to help?"

Sari was able to smile. "No, thanks. It's nothing. I was reminded of where I grew up, that's all."

"Well, that's a very natural feeling. So, I take it that this is your first visit to our beautiful Southwest."

"Yes, it's my first." And it will be my last, Sari thought as she gritted her teeth. "Do you know a place called Prescott? My paternal—in fact, my only—grandmother lives there."

"Really? So do I. Perhaps we're acquainted. What's her name?"

"Her maiden name was Hudspith, and her first husband was a Wyatt. Now she has one of those British double names connected with a hyphen: Griffith-Rhys."

The elderly passenger beamed. "Talk about a small world. She is well known in Prescott; in fact, we serve together on the Yavapai College Auxiliary Board. I often run into your grandmother in town." Opening her purse, she brought out a calling card. "Here's my telephone number. If I can do anything for you while you're here, please don't hesitate to give me a call."

Though Sari doubted there would be any reason to get in touch, she thanked the woman and tucked the card in her pocket. She wondered what this nice stranger would say if she were to confess that she hadn't the faintest clue why the arrogant grandmother who had never been more than a shadow hovering in the wings of her life had sent for her. After all, Sari thought, as soon as I've said the things I've wanted to say to her for years, I'll be heading straight back to the East Coast.

The seat belt sign came on and the Captain's voice boomed over the intercom. "Welcome to Phoenix," he drawled. "We've made excellent time and we'll be landing at Sky Harbor in ten minutes. It's a gorgeous day in the Valley of the Sun. Have a good one."

With a reminder to relay her greetings, her grandmother's friend collected her own luggage and left Sari waiting to be met in the baggage area. Three quarters of an hour later, Sari was still standing alone by the carousel when a man came striding down the empty corridor. He frowned as he parked himself in front of her.

"Miss Wyatt?" The deep voice rumbled as she looked up at the tall rangy fellow who held a Stetson in one hand and mopped his brow with the other. "I'm terribly embarrassed to be so late but I got tied up in traffic. I apologize. Your flight was smooth, I hope?"

"Oh yes, it was fine. And you must be my grandmother's chauffeur—" Distracted by the unreadable expression that crossed his tanned face, Sari stammered, "Oh dear, have I made a mistake?"

"No, you're right on. I am the chauffeur."

Dressed more like a ranch hand, he looked good in his Levi's, western shirt, and boots. With a penetrating glance from his brown eyes and a reserved smile on a rather severe mouth beneath a full mustache, he said, "I'm Montegue. But hey, everybody knows better than to call me that. Plain 'Monty' will do just fine."

She extended her hand. "I appreciate your meeting me, Monty."

"Actually, this really is just a bit of good luck, since we thought we'd be seeing you on Friday. Tuesday's the day I spend in the Valley on business, and when I dropped in at the lawyer's office this afternoon they told me that Jessica—my wife—had called to say she just learned that you'd moved your flight up to today."

Sari shrugged. "Yes. Since I was told it would be all right to make any change of plans that suited me better, that's what I did." She did not think she needed to share with the chauffeur that this command appearance offered the opportunity to escape, if only temporarily, to a place where she wouldn't run into Michael Hancock.

She wrinkled her forehead. "I don't understand why you didn't get my wire sooner."

"It's because your grandmother lives out in the boonies. Whenever there's trouble with the lines, like with the heavy storms we've been having lately, we're always the last to get service." He lifted her bag and pressed the elevator button. "Shall we go?"

When Sari didn't move, he paused and reached into his wallet for his I.D. "I see you've lived too long in wild and wooly New York City to go riding off over the sagebrush with a fellow you just met. I congratulate you; you're a very wise young lady."

As they stepped into the elevator, she thought about his I.D. There was something odd about it. The picture was his all right, but like an elusive mouse, the faint impression scampered across her mind. But she was too late; it got away. She had no reason—did she?—to doubt Monty, yet she wished she could scan that identification card again.

Emerging onto the top level of the parking lot, they were hit by a blast of air so hot that she quickly removed her coat. "I left home in the middle of a premature cold snap," she said. "So I guess I brought all the wrong things for Arizona."

But it didn't really matter. This was only a minor discomfort that would be forgotten as soon as she had the satisfaction of facing her grandmother. And it shouldn't be long now. According to Monty, the trip to her place would take only a couple of hours.

As it turned out, they picked up another passenger who would help to make the time fly. He was lounging against an expensive-looking white limousine parked in solitary splendor in the corner of the lot. As they approached, he looked Sari over and said with a twinkle in his eye, "Monty, how about an introduction?"

With an exclamation of pleasure, the driver held up his hand. "Ron! Give me five! Say, this is great. Sari, this young guy is my wife's cousin, Ron Cooper. And Ron, meet Sari Wyatt." He wagged his head. "You are as transparent as glass, Ron. You found out I was meeting her, didn't you?"

"Yeah. When I called Jessica, she said Sari was coming in, so I figured this might be a good chance to pay you all a visit."

Golden-flecked eyes twinkled down at Sari from about six feet two as he added, "You know what? I think I'm right."

"So where's your rig?"

"I left her in the garage over on Van Buren. I found out the air-conditioning system needs an overhaul, so I have time to kill. If you don't object, Sari, I'll ride up with you and Monty."

She wanted to pull away from the hand that had fastened in a proprietary manner on her elbow. She had always avoided men like Ron—men who are good-looking and know it.

This one, who was probably in his late twenties, was incredible from the crown of his blond, curly perm to the thick lashes that opened wide when he laughed to reveal those topaz glints; to an even blonder, carefully-trimmed mustache; and, finally, the tawny hairs on his muscular arms. Ron Cooper added up to a golden, well-groomed specimen, and he made Sari nervous.

He held on until her suitcase and carry-on were stowed in the trunk and his duffel tossed in after them. Then, with a sweeping gesture, Ron handed her into the car. She felt as though she had been dropped onto a blue plush marshmallow.

This was the first time she had been in a luxury automobile and a quick glance told her it was all here: cleverly-concealed reading lights, stereo speakers, a well-stocked bar that included crystal glasses, and the inevitable sliding window between front and back, which Monty left open.

"This Rolls is okay but you haven't seen anything yet," Ron assured Sari. "Wait until you get a load of your grandmother's Jeep Cherokee. She had it custom made and it's a woman's car. Outside, pale orange with brown trim; inside, fully-upholstered in apricot. Fur, no less."

Over his shoulder, as they left the airport complex for the northbound freeway, Monty nodded. "There's a lot of rough terrain in the area and she handles that four-wheel drive like a real pro. But why don't you tell Sari about your outfit, Ron? It doesn't have a pastel interior, but it sure has more wheels."

"You can say that again. Eighteen of 'em. Plus, I've got CB equipment, even a sleeping compartment behind the cab. And lots of chrome. In other words, the works."

He sounded so proud that Sari felt herself unbending. "I see. So you're a truck driver."

"Lady, lady, it's not just a truck. It's a tractor trailer and there's all the difference in the world. I'm what's called in the trade an 'independent'—that's a freelancer—and my territory is the whole enchilada—the good old U.S.A., from coast to coast, north to south, wherever I can pick up a job."

Ron cocked his head. "I love my rig but I really don't mind being without my own transportation at the moment. I'm always glad to see your grandma. She is quite a woman. But of course you already know that."

"No," Sari responded flatly, "I didn't know that. I've never met my grandmother."

Ron's eyebrows drew together in a golden arch, but

he made no comment on Sari's admission. Instead, he tapped the chauffeur and said, "Mont, she's the spitting image of the Duchess. Those high cheek bones, her green-blue eyes; they have that same sexy little slant at the corners. And, of course, the red hair. Very like, don't you agree?"

"Oh come on," Sari protested. "And who, if I may ask, is this Duchess person I'm supposed to resemble?"

In the rear view mirror, Sari saw Monty's eyes narrow. "Why, your grandmother, of course. Oliver, her second husband, was a duke, the Duke of Rhysbury. He was an odd one, though, because while he was British—staid old Welsh family from Llangollen—Oliver Griffith-Rhys wasn't wild about having people kowtow to him. He didn't use his title, nor allow anyone else to do so. Nevertheless, your grandmother is a legitimate duchess. Nobody ever told you?"

She shook her head. Her father's mother was a duchess? "It's news to me." Rather shocking news. But on second thought, Sari wasn't too surprised to learn her grandmother belonged to the exclusive circle of nobility.

This duchess no doubt met every requirement. Apparently, if the Rolls Royce was any indication, she had a plentiful share of this world's goods. She fit in. But there was nothing noble about this woman who, years ago, had disinherited her own flesh and blood. She had not allowed her missionary son even one shilling during the lean years he spent in India. And all because he had refused to let her orchestrate his life for him.

Chapter Two

Sari managed to speak over the lump in her throat. "I notice your accent. Monty. Are you English, too?"

"Yes. However, I had no lineage whatsoever to brag about when the Duchess found me wandering in the alleys of Liverpool and on a whim took me under her wing. That was fourteen years ago."

"She's the reason our Montegue has such a high-falutin' name," Ron explained. "The Duchess didn't think the one he had was classy enough so she changed it."

Sari was glad Monty's attention had turned to inserting a new tape and adjusting the volume on the background music he apparently preferred—Country Western. She needed a moment to digest this information. So her grandmother had picked a boy out of the gutter and made a gentleman of him? She had had time for a stranger, but not her son. How kind of her!

That homeless ragamuffin, now transformed into a proper chauffeur seated at the controls of a vehicle that cost a small fortune, gestured toward the mountains rippling above the horizon on the left. "Sari, we've left

Metropolitan Phoenix far behind us now and your grandmother's home is over there. Northwest, to be exact.

"It's off the beaten track in a part of the state where there used to be a lot of mines. Gold, silver, and copper. Many of those diggings were abandoned for one reason or another. They are so numerous that it's impossible to seal them all off, even if you could locate them." He shook his head. "The shafts are deep. They are treacherous traps to anyone who goes tramping carelessly about."

"Really?" Sari was only half listening to the driver. She was covertly observing the man beside her who was trying to hold her hand. Some sixth sense was cautioning Sari about Ron Cooper.

"No problem," he reassured Monty. "Sari won't run into any trouble because I'll be looking after her. I plan on occupying all of her time."

Ron smiled warmly. "Let's talk about something fun. First, do you really dig New York? You know, Sari, you look like a nice, quiet gal who'd be afraid of her own shadow. I can't see you knocking around the Big Apple all alone—" Ron pulled her against him. "Hey, no offense! I was only kidding."

"It's all right." She had stiffened, but her reaction had nothing to do with Ron's chauvinistic appraisal. It was his mention of New York that had flashed pictures into her mind. Pictures of Michael Hancock.

To blot them out, Sari closed her eyes and squeezed her hands tightly together so she wouldn't see how bare the fourth finger on her left hand looked. This morning she had taken off Michael's engagement ring and she would never put it on again. So why did she feel as if she were still wearing it?

I should have told Michael long ago how I felt, she thought sadly. And she told herself again that they would have been spared so much pain if only her supervisor, a year ago, had chosen someone else to represent the Upper Manhattan Crisis Center on the Mayor's Target Commission.

Sari had been thrilled to be a part of that elite group dealing with the growing problem of crimes against women. And as they gathered for their first brainstorming session, Sari had sensed immediately why Michael, in spite of his youth, was the Mayor's candidate to spearhead the project.

She had found herself captivated by the sincerity that was apparent in the man with rumpled hair and a craggy profile, whose radio and television ministry was making him a household name in the five boroughs.

Amused, Sari had watched the expressions on the faces of the other female members of the group who, obviously, were also touched by Michael's charisma. All of them—Sari included—hung on his words, but she was flattered at meeting's end to be the one he cornered at the door.

To her surprise, this media personality, who possessed a silver tongue when facing the camera, came across as quite shy when he asked if Sari cared to join him for a cup of coffee.

"I, uh, I know this neat little Mom 'n Pop's place around the corner from the Plaza," he told her, "and I could use a pick-me-up about now. Not to mention a big piece of their delicious apple strudel! Is it possible, well, could I interest you in going with me?"

"Why, thanks," she had said. "I'd like that very much."

As they started down Broadway, he groaned and stopped suddenly in the middle of the sidewalk. "Oh boy! I walk whenever I get the chance and I didn't ask if you minded hiking clear downtown. I apologize. I'll get a cab."

Sari laughed. "Please don't. I enjoy walking."

He had seemed pleased with her response and was still smiling when they were seated at a table by the window of the coffee shop. "I just realized this is the first time I've invited someone to share 'my' table."

His finger followed the pattern of the gingham cloth as he shrugged self-consciously. "You'd be surprised at how many ideas for sermons I get as I sit here watching the stream of humanity flow by."

"You sound like a poet."

"Of sorts, I guess. But I think I'm more of a fighter, like when I can be involved in something like this Target Commission. After all, I have the greatest example to follow. When He was here on earth, Christ was a champion of the underdog, and that's what I want to be."

Later, when she and Michael had started dating, she knew this man with a voice that was like organ tones was someone she could learn to love—one who would cherish her as her father had cherished her mother.

From her, Sari had picked up the English expression, "over the moon," but she hadn't really known what it meant until the night she and Michael had returned from a concert at Lincoln Center and strolled toward her apartment near Riverside Drive.

Pointing to a marble bench in front of one of the large apartment buildings, Michael had said, "This is a nice quiet spot. I don't think the doorman will mind if we sit here for a minute. I've got something to show you."

His hazel eyes twinkled as he reached into his pocket and brought out a small jeweler's box. "This was my mom's engagement ring that she left to me. She told me this is for that special girl I would ask to be my wife. I love you, Sari Wyatt, and I'm asking you to do me the honor of marrying me."

Tears blinded her and her hands shook so hard Michael had to help her lift the lid of the tiny box. Then he got out his handkerchief and dried her eyes so she could see the gold band set with rubies and diamonds. Now she knew what that silly expression was all about. "Oh Michael, I'm over the moon with happiness! Of course I'll marry you."

"God has given me a childlike faith," he had confessed shyly. "Every morning when I wake up I remind myself that God is a God of miracles and I'll trust Him for one that day." Enfolding her hands in his, Michael had added, "That's why I believe our meeting a year ago was no accident. Our paths were divinely foreordained to cross. It was all in God's perfect plan."

Sari had wanted to believe it. She had wanted to believe the joy she had found would go on forever, but slowly, over the months, she began to cringe inside whenever she thought of the disparity between Michael and herself. Even though he seemed to be unaware of its existence, Sari was all too aware that it was there. She felt the gulf was widening each time she listened to Michael preach about the love of God.

Michael was utterly committed to his Lord while she was being consumed by the malice she was hanging onto—a destructive force directed at the individual who had decreed that her only son and his family did not exist. Her grandmother.

With her poisoned thoughts bottled up inside, Sari tossed restlessly through sleepless nights. Though countless other hurting people sought Michael Hancock's sympathetic counsel, she could not bare her heart before him. She could not bring herself to ask for his advice. Besides, she already knew what Michael would say about the loathing that fettered her and the gnawing animosity that was undermining her happiness. She could hear him: "Sari, darling, it's not worth it! Give it up. Ask God to help you."

"Nobody can help me," she told herself, "not even God." It was an alien way to feel about the One she had once called her friend. And she had to face the fact that she really did not want to be rid of her burning desire for revenge. Not even for Michael.

Michael was God's dedicated servant. He needed a

wife who could be a true helpmate—one whose spirit was at peace, not war. "And he deserves better than me," Sari had admitted to herself. Breaking their engagement would be the greatest favor she could ever do for him.

It was while she was trying to steel herself to break the news to Michael that the Duchess' summons reached her. How ironic that its arrival should be so perfectly-timed, just when she needed to get away. Away from Michael.

Before leaving for JFK that morning, she had tucked the heirloom engagement ring back into its satin-lined nest, enclosed a short letter, and sent the package by special messenger to Michael's office.

She was ashamed for taking a coward's way out, but at least it was done, and all she felt was relief. She told herself again that breaking off was for the best, and one day Michael would thank her. He would get over it. And so would she.

Abruptly, Sari returned to the here and now as Ron gently nudged her and she opened her eyes. His face came into focus as he smiled at her and pointed through the window of the limousine. "Look there, Sari, that's Cordes Junction up ahead. That's where we leave the freeway."

"Right. If we'd stayed on the Black Canyon, we would eventually reach Flagstaff," Monty added. "Flag—as many Arizonans affectionately call it—is a town with a true Indian flavor. You can see native Americans on the streets and it's the gateway to the Grand Canyon."

Though lapsing into frequent periods of preoccupied silence, Monty had proven to be a well-informed guide. The names of desert plants—yucca, ocotillo, saguaro—rolled off his tongue, and he identified by name the small settlements where houses huddled together as though they still feared an attack by gangs of outlaws.

"An interesting side trip many folks like to take is to

Oak Creek Canyon to check out the red rock formations that have made that area so famous," Monty said. "And you have to see TLAQUEPAQUE, the artist's paradise."

Ron nodded. "That's just one of the touristy places the Duchess will be showing you."

Sari wanted to bark, "I think not! I won't be staying around here any longer than necessary!" But she bit her lip and said nothing.

"Have you noticed the topography is changing? We're getting into ponderosa country," Monty said. "You'll have to see Prescott some other day because we'll pass it up for now. It's a thriving little metropolis. Prescott was Arizona's first capital and the Court House is a historical landmark. There are other buildings also, which out-of-towners rave about, but I decided to take a more scenic route. There are some fantastic mountains in the neighborhood. Spruce, the one closest to your grandmother's home, will be coming up soon."

As they pulled out of a steep climb, Monty angled the car onto the wide shoulder. "We'll stop on this lay-by for a minute so you can see the Prescott National Forest, recognized as some of the most beautiful land in the entire Southwest."

Sari could believe it. The panorama was so breathtaking that her negative feelings about being there faded for the moment. Arizona was painted with the soft beiges and tans of the desert's flat spaces, and now these slopes and valleys appeared in every shade of green.

Then, unexpectedly, she saw something that caused her to blink her eyes. "If I didn't know better, I'd say that's a castle, complete with towers and turrets. But of course that's silly. There are no castles here."

Ron agreed. "Right-o. How could that be?"

Sari squinted through her sunglasses. "Then what is it?"

"Don't listen to him. It is a castle. And really," Monty said smugly, "why is that so far-fetched? This state has several of them, one of which happens to be perched on the south side of Camelback Mountain. You could have seen Camelback as your plane came in to touch down at Sky Harbor. That particular castle was designed by a Phoenix dentist—a man who had always been intrigued by the idea of actually living in a castle. He had it built to specification, and it is Moorish in design, really unique. The one you see in the near distance is unique, too, and in a class of its own."

The air was so clear that Sari could make out the details, even from miles away. "Look at that drum tower! That was the 'keep' in olden days. See the skinny apertures on the sides? The castle defenders used to dump boiling oil through those openings down onto the heads of invaders. I never thought I'd see battlements like those all along the top, with the solid 'merlons' to stand behind. And isn't that a weird rectangular tower with twin turrets? Oh my, I . . ." Her voice failed. She had stepped into the Middle Ages and was overcome with emotion.

"Wow. You sure know a lot about castles!" Ron said. "You must read a lot."

"Yes, I do. All my life. M.K.'s—missionary kids—for lack of other diversions, devour books. I loved fairy tales and stories of knights in shining armor. Anything historical. And you'd be amazed at how much you can absorb from an encyclopedia." Sari frowned, "Stop smiling, you two. I'm serious! As for castles, somewhere along the way, they just became my thing. So, since you insist this one is not a figment of my imagination, tell me, do they open it for viewing?"

"It may be off the beaten path but the travel agents here in the Southwest regularly bring day-trippers out here. So it's always open. You wouldn't like to see it?"

"What a question. Oh, Monty, would I!"

He began the descent, with Sari twisting to keep in sight the astonishing sight of a castle in the wilderness.

Reaching a stretch of highway where it widened with antique shops on one side and an old-fashioned schoolhouse on the other, they veered left. They were on a winding track that doubled back onto a partially-paved road, then dipped into an arroyo and bounced up the opposite bank.

Even if the Rolls Royce had not been so well cushioned, Sari would not have felt the bumps. She was on the edge of the seat with her face pressed against the window when the imposing structure set against a backdrop of pine-covered slopes came into full view.

She felt like pinching herself. It couldn't be, but it was: a real castle, a jewel in a setting of emerald green. It had been placed here, most likely by a crazy eccentric with a flair for the bizarre, along with overflowing coffers to indulge his fancies.

To Sari's educated eye it was obvious that the old had been freely mixed with the new. "It's a hodge-podge. Stone walls. Elegant bay windows. Romeo and Juliet balconies. And instead of a moat, they have a...a swimming pool!"

Dropping into a narrow valley, then up again, they approached along a drive paved with cobblestones and lined with graceful silvery cottonwoods. Slowing to a crawl, the limousine skirted the crescent-shaped pool and Monty stopped at the foot of wide steps. Sari felt as though she had skittered into a time warp. To the tape deck's accompaniment of a twanging guitar and a sorrowful cowpoke mourning his lost love, Sari realized what was actually happening. It was a magical moment. And it was happening to her.

She looked up at the enormous nail-studded door that was not unlike the portcullis of the thirteenth century. She watched as it swung open and the castle staff came parading down. They were resplendent, nattily decked out in matching outfits that were more than mere costume party uniforms worn to lend local color.

The men wore practical jeans and short-sleeved shirts and the women were dressed in skirts or culottes and lace-trimmed blouses. And everything was in a vibrant shade of blue.

"That's a sizable lineup," Sari said in a low voice. "In fact, it bears out an article I read recently. It talked about the plight of so many owners of castles and manors in Britain. In order to beat the rising cost of upkeep, they're conducting tours of the premises. Some have even turned their homes into bed-and-breakfasts. You can't deny it's a clever way to be able to keep on living in such splendor." She smiled at the sight of the group standing at attention.

"I feel like applauding! Do they stage this little demonstration for every eager tourist who drops by?"

"I doubt you can put it off any longer," the younger man told the driver. "You've got to tell her."

"Tell me what?" Sari demanded.

Monty turned to face her. She couldn't read the expression in his dark eyes but he looked serious, as though what he was about to say might have a drastic effect upon her life.

Instinctively, she braced herself.

Chapter Three

"I see it hasn't dawned on you," Monty began. "Sari, this is not an ordinary castle. It's a copy of the Duchess' childhood home in Northumberland. The Castle Hudspith. After your grandmother married in her late teens, she made her headquarters in London, which would be the house in Mayfair. She was especially partial to the old homestead, however, and the family always spent half of every year there."

He sounded more than ever like a tour guide as he continued, "Hudspith Castle had been constructed over the ruins of a Roman amphitheater soon after the Norman Conquest. It was rebuilt and modified several times, the last during the 1800's. Of course, this facsimile was made somewhat smaller and, as you've already noticed, there are a number of interesting changes. Sari, do you understand? This is your grandma's home."

Ron grinned. "So what do you think? Are you surprised?"

Sari gasped. For her, it was the understatement of all time.

What she had just learned stunned Sari. This magnificent citadel was a domicile worthy of a queen. Or a duchess. Her heart gave a painful lurch, and she winced as she realized that her father must have known all about the castle in Northumberland. He spent much of his life there, yet he never told her.

Her eyes burned with tears of regret for all the things he could have shared but must have been too hurt to talk about. Sari clenched her teeth. The sooner she confronted the party responsible for that unnatural state of affairs, the better.

She thought she was ready when Monty hopped out and offered to help her from the car. "Would you mind going down the line and shaking hands?" he asked. "Some of the staff are from the old country and enjoy a bit of pomp and ceremony. And sure, I admit I do, too."

As she followed his directions, the staff greeted her with the dignity and aplomb that is like a second skin Britishers never seem to shed. But after they dispersed, she turned, searching for something, anything, to delay the inevitable meeting.

Sari knew why she was stalling for time. It was because she had wanted to be cool and collected, but now her resentment was nearing the boiling point. What if she burst into maudlin tears of frustration when at last she and her grandmother met?

"Here's Jessica," Monty said as he waved Sari toward the petite young woman who was watching from the doorway. "Come meet my wife."

"Howdy, Sari," Jessica drawled. "I'm glad to see you made it." She was adorable, from the top of her head with its tousled crown of Little Orphan Annie curls, to her designer jeans and her pointy-toed cowgirl boots. Sari noticed the sporty locket suspended around her neck on a delicate golden chain. It was made in the shape of the state of Arizona with a tiny gold nugget inset in the northwest quadrant. Sari, who had expected Monty's wife to be very English, knew this was no transplanted British lass. Jessica was all Westerner. "I'm the unofficial housekeeper here, so let me welcome you to Hudspith Castle."

She smiled and then ushered Sari into what would have been called in olden days the Great Hall. Sari was immediately transfixed by the central object.

It was the giant figure of a beautifully-executed golden eagle mounted on the front of a twelve-foot-tall mantel. Jessica, at Sari's elbow, nodded. "This bird is your grandmother's pride and joy. And with good reason. Her family dates back to antiquity, which is when they took the eagle for their crest."

As she moved closer, Sari was dazzled by the splendor of the sapphires and opals that formed the letters around the coat of arms. They spelled out the creed in Latin around the top and in English at the bottom. In a hushed voice she repeated them: "Valor, Endurance, Loyalty." Oh, superb!

Monty started down the length of the chamber with its walls covered with exquisite murals. Sari fell into step beside him for what seemed like a stroll through a museum. They walked past statues and book stands that displayed large gold-bound volumes spread open. There was even a massive set of armor standing guard at each end of the room.

"The castle's laid out in the shape of a square-bottomed U," Monty told her. "And this room fills up more than half of the central area."

They emerged through glass doors onto a broad terrace from which the wings on either side stretched ahead. The left wing, curiously enough, was only two stories tall, with a rectangular tower. The wing on the right had three floors with the drum tower at the front. It was an original type of design that should have made the building look unbalanced. Instead, Sari thought it presented a charming, slightly offbeat effect.

"The 'old timers' in the area still tell stories about mines that were on this property. Later, it was used for a summer campground—very nice with its hills and valleys. Eventually, the government traded it for some of the Duchess' real estate in the southeastern part of Arizona," Monty said. "There, beyond the castle's left wing is a drop-off that levels to flat terrain. The kennels of the guard dogs are beneath the west wing."

She could not repress a shiver. He smiled reassuringly. "Oh, there's no need to fear these dogs. With our famous Arizona heat, the dogs stay inside during the daytime and only run at night from about two o'clock on. Even then, they only bother some stranger who may be skulking about."

She shivered again. "My philosophy concerning all canines is one of live-and-let-live. I don't trust any dog. And I can tell you I won't be revising my attitude, ever."

From what she had seen from the mountain lookout, Sari already knew there would be no completely-enclosed courtyard, and the absence of this—the bailey—was one of the major alterations. This allowed for a lovely vista of lawns and hedges that beckoned through the open space at the far end of the yard. And closer in on a flower-bordered island of decorative rock stood an old-fashioned summerhouse. A gazebo.

Its latticed sides were festooned with rambler roses climbing to a pagoda roof. But its outstanding feature was the weather vane that swung lazily to and fro atop its apex—a rounder, fleshed-out edition of the majestic eagle she had seen in the great hall.

From aristocratic beak to golden-tipped feathers gleaming in the late afternoon sunshine, it was unlike any weather vane Sari had ever seen. Monty noticed her reaction. "I guess you could say the Duchess has a penchant for eagles and just had to have one on their summerhouse. This is a favorite haunt and of course the Duke designed everything in it. Who else would stick a chess table in the middle of a gazebo? Leave it to Oliver Griffith-Rhys to think of that."

As they retraced their steps toward Jessica and her cousin, Sari glanced up at the gallery that ran around all four sides of the great hall at the second story level. Suspended from the vaulted ceiling was a chandelier with clusters of shimmery crystal droplets that looked like thousands of sparkling bits of light from a skyrocket bursting into a shower of diamond stars.

When Monty pressed a switch flooding the room with light, Sari was convinced of one thing: this was the castle of anyone's dreams. Especially Sari Wyatt's.

What she could do without was the one who owned it all. She sighed and gave herself a mental shake. She was here on business, and she would get on with it.

"Jessica, where is she?" Sari asked. "Is my grandmother waiting upstairs for me?"

"I hate to tell you this. She's not here. She has disappeared."

Jessica's announcement caused her husband's mouth to narrow to an unsmiling gash. "That's not funny, Jess. Quit the kidding and tell us, where is she?"

"I have told you. She isn't here. I've looked. If you doubt me, look for yourself."

"But that's preposterous, and you know it. The Duchess would never take off when she knew Sari was coming today."

"That's just it. She didn't know. She was outside with her dogs, trimming the roses on the gazebo—that was about ten o'clock—when Sari's message was finally phoned in. By the time I got hold of you at Oscar's office and then went out to give the Duchess the news, she was gone. One minute she and the dogs were there; then it's as if the ground opened and swallowed them up."

Ron laughed. "You can't be serious!"

"Jessica, pardon me, but people just don't vanish without a trace," Sari objected. "There has to be a logical explanation."

She was cut short by the squeal of tires followed by

the noise of a car door slamming. There was the pounding of feet up the stone steps. Suddenly she was looking at one of the roundest, shortest, men she had ever seen. This middle-aged man had that kind of cheerful, running-over-with-jolly countenance that immediately dispels gloom.

"See what I brought us!" His arms were loaded with bakery boxes that he shifted uneasily when he received no response. "What goes on? You all look as if something terrible has happened."

"Oscar," Ron said, "we don't know where the Duchess is."

The jollies faded abruptly. "You don't mean she's missing? So what has been done to find her?"

"We just got here ourselves and, as you can see, this is Sari."

The newcomer gave her a searching glance from his deep-set eyes, then pulled off his horn-rimmed glasses. He dropped the boxes onto a Louis XV table and extended both hands. "Hello, Sari, my dear. I'm Oscar Drayton, your grandmother's Phoenix attorney. I'm the one who contacted you, and I do apologize for the peremptory sound of the telegram I sent. I am very glad you're here, however, and I deeply regret meeting you under these circumstances. I feel there must be some mistake. Your grandma has disappeared? Rubbish!"

"But she did. Why do you doubt me?" Jessica's lips tightened. "I got the whole crew out to look for her, and they scoured the property. She was there by the gazebo and it was like, now you see her, now you don't. Monty, please don't give me that look. She's not here!"

Following Jessica's bizarre announcement of the Duchess' disappearance, a glacial chill seemed to fall on the group. Sari felt it and suspected the others felt it as well. Especially the chauffeur, whose shocked expression had intensified. "I don't like it," Monty mumbled. "Not one bloody bit."

"Of course you don't. However, life must go on, which includes a special dinner—a 'company' menu in Sari's honor. Roast beef, Yorkshire pudding and all the calorie-laden trimmings. While you take up her bags, I'll check on things in the kitchen." Jessica shrugged, "It's just like a funeral; no matter what, you still have to eat."

To Sari, who had picked at the food served on the plane, roast beef sounded delicious, but she did not blame Monty for glaring at his wife for her poor choice of words. Making no move to do as she said, he seemed to be in deep thought. His broad forehead furrowed and one hand tugged at a corner of his heavy mustache.

"I am going to sound the dinner gong early. For heaven's sake, Monty, go!" Jessica's command was sharp.

He wagged his head and motioned Sari toward the wide archway leading to a graceful curving staircase. She hung back. "Wait. I...there has to be a reason, there must be. People just don't. Disappear, you know. Perhaps you've forgotten some remark she made about going into town to the store. Or the beauty shop."

"On foot? The garage was the very first place we checked, and the Jeep is still there." The housekeeper's tone took on an edge of exasperation. "Sari, forgive me, but your grandmother is, how shall I phrase it, a free spirit. It's just the way she is, which is why I am not about to waste time worrying about her."

There was nothing to do but trail Monty up the thickly-carpeted steps. "See you later, Ron. Mr. Drayton." Sari was anything but calm, even as she conceded that the seething emotions in her mind were not colored by any filial concern. Not a shred! She certainly didn't care about what might have happened to this delinquent grandparent.

However, her disappearance was already affecting Sari. She had been psychologically fortified for a meeting, yet all the questions and righteous indignation must now be placed on hold.

She felt oddly deflated and sensed a corresponding slump on Monty's part. He had worn an air of dejection ever since the report of his employer's absence. He offered no conversation as they reached the gallery, turned left, then right, then right once more—or was it left? She feared she would never be able to find her way back downstairs.

The castle that had seemed so charming now assumed a gloomy atmosphere that was heightened by the dimness of the corridors through which Monty led her. The sole illumination was candle-shaped bulbs. The shadows cast by them were eerie. Sari felt threatened. She shivered, thinking that if the lights were suddenly extinguished, these passages would be as dark as midnight.

The chauffeur glanced over his shoulder to see what was slowing her down. What if she told him that she was nervous about being shut away in a strange room where the isolation would give her goose bumps?

Then something happened to change the picture: Marianne appeared on the scene.

Curled up on a deacon's bench in a small hallway with a carved door at the end, one of the English maids was waiting for their arrival. About Sari's age, she had a piquant heart-shaped face and dimples in her bright rosy cheeks.

She dropped a deep curtsy, then giggled. "We don't do that here as a general rule, but it's fun. I thought, well, I'm sort of at loose ends with the Duchess gone missing, and I'm looking for something to do. I hoped Miss Wyatt might allow me to help with settling in."

Sari could have hugged this girl with the cornflower blue eyes and ingenuous smile. "How nice! As you can see, I'm traveling light, but I'd be grateful if you'd show me where to put my things." She added, "To tell the truth, I'd be very glad to have some company."

"Good, then it's mutual." Monty pushed open the door and waved the two women into a room that could have been lifted out of any of the illustrated story books that had been Sari's childhood companions.

Marianne beamed. "Isn't this lovely? It's so quaint and old-fashioned. Have you ever stayed in a round room before?"

Apparently, the maid's cheerful manner had done something for Monty. He was almost smiling. "You're standing in the drum tower, Sari," he said.

Chapter Four

The chauffeur crossed the colorful wall-to-wall braided rag rug to open a pair of glass doors. "Your balcony. It's large enough to accommodate a hammock and has a view of the drive and swimming pool."

"The rest of this west wing is unoccupied at present and the third floor, including the tower room above this one, is closed off," Marianne told her. "Do you think you will be all right here in your ivory tower?"

Sari grinned. "All right? A person would have to be crazy not to love this room." She had already forgotten the apprehension she'd experienced just a short time ago.

The chauffeur deposited Sari's suitcase on a stand and turned to the maid. "Okay, then, I'll shove off. It was thoughtful of you to lend our visitor a hand, Marianne. Thanks for being so considerate."

She was also sensitive, Sari learned. Quietly, Marianne began placing Sari's belongings in the wardrobe and dresser, leaving Sari to inspect the extra touches that made this bedroom so unique.

She exclaimed over the cherry wood curio cabinet that was shaped like a hollow log and housed a family of carved, miniature owls, the desk with writing paper and pens, and the dressing table and bench with flounced skirts of the same organdy fabric that made up the canopy and curtains of the four-poster bed.

When she raised a questioning glance over the graceful table located beside a wicker chaise lounge, Marianne nodded. "That's a Marie Antoinette chocolate table. There by the bed is a matching candlestand."

Nearby, there was a deep armchair upholstered in a watermelon shade to complement the pale pink of the drapes on the doors. And, as if that were not enough, a wide bay window seat beckoned.

Sari sank against its pile of pillows and smiled at Marianne who said, "I know. It really gets to you. Everything is outmoded, but it's so cute, the exact way the Duchess' tower bedroom in Northumberland was decorated. She has her comfy digs in the east wing, but can you believe she comes over here and spends whole days? I guess she plays her old records and sits in that window seat. Would you mind if I say something?"

"Not at all. Please, go ahead."

"First of all, I love your grandma dearly, and I probably know her as well as anyone here, excepting Monty, of course. For all her wealth and position, she is still an empty person. She has a longing for joy and real contentment, but no matter where she has gone, she has never found it. She gets beautiful things and beautiful people around her and still she's not happy."

When there was no comment from Sari, Marianne continued. "Miss Wyatt, from what Monty told us, you and the Duchess are strangers. When you get to know her, you'll see she is quite alone. I guess you think that's a nervy thing to say, especially about a duchess, but I really do care about her."

This new side of her grandmother surprised Sari. But, unlike Marianne who actually had tears in her eyes, she felt no pity. The woman didn't have to be alone, ever, she reminded herself. She could have had my father and after he died she could have had me. But she didn't even care enough to answer my letter.

The maid jumped as the cuckoo called from the clock above the desk. "Oh, oh. Look at the time! Miss Wyatt, if you hurry, you can still have a bubble bath before dinner. The bathroom is stocked with all sorts of potions and colognes and fluffy towels."

"I'd love that. But let's dispense with this 'Miss' business. I've noticed that 'casual' is the word here, so please call me Sari."

"All right, if you really want me to," Marianne answered happily. She went to turn on the water. "I'll be back in thirty minutes. I imagine you could do with a little guidance, right?"

Sari was left staring at the tub. Resting on claw feet, it was ridiculously huge, but size was only one of its unusual features. Someone with up-to-date ideas had been at work here. This bathtub in a room with mirrored walls and glass shelves served a dual purpose: with a flip of a switch Sari could enjoy her own personal whirlpool.

But this was her grandmother's home, her dainty bedroom, her mod bathroom. Sari hated touching any of it. She twisted her lips and thought she really should repack her things and hightail it out of there.

However, as she soaked in the warm fragrant water, she began to change her mind. The chance to explore an authentic castle most certainly would never come her way again. Why spoil it by acting like a child.

She blow-dried her hair, then stood at the wardrobe, trying to decide which of her three dresses to wear. She had to admit she could not leave if she wanted to. She was enraptured with the Castle Hudspith. She was under its spell. The least she could do was relax and just maybe she would enjoy her short visit.

Enjoy? Sari winced.

After she slipped into the autumn-colored A-line with the gold and green scarf, she swept her wavy hair to one side and pulled a few tendrils against her cheek. "Come in, it's open," she called when she heard a light knock on the door.

Marianne appeared. She froze. "Oh..." she breathed.

"What's the matter?"

The rosy face reflected in the mirror above the dressing table wore a bemused expression. "My goodness, but you gave me a start. You are so pretty, just like the Duchess in that color. Like her portrait in the gallery. Come, I'll show you."

The faces in the gilded frames arranged along the gallery wall stared impassively at Sari in the glow of recessed lighting. "These are Hudspith Royals," Marianne proudly declared. "Plus the Duchess' two husbands."

Sari had no trouble spotting her grandmother. It was just like looking at Sari Wyatt wearing the bobbed hairdo of the Roaring Twenties and with the same up-tilted eyes Ron had noticed.

"See what I mean?" Marianne whispered.

Feeling sick, Sari turned away and, misunderstanding completely, the maid nodded. "Yes, I can see how it would affect you. It's unreal, the resemblance. Especially when you think that how she looks now is most likely how you will look at her age. And Sari, that's not an unpleasant prospect. At seventy-something, she's a handsome woman."

The muted sound of the gong floated up to them and Marianne left. Sari felt unaccountably disturbed. This was the first portrait of her grandmother she had ever seen, and it was all she could do to keep from succumbing to the caustic thoughts that were never far from the surface of her mind.

As she reached the landing and started down the stairway, she saw a tall figure standing at the bottom and for a moment her world seemed to slide sideways. But it wasn't Michael Hancock waiting for her in the hall below...it was only Ron Cooper, an admiring golden man who whistled appreciatively as he tucked her hand under his arm and ushered her into the formal dining room.

A magnificent candle-lighted trestle table gleamed with heavy silver and gold-rimmed china. Monty, Jessica, and Mr. Drayton huddled in a corner of the room. When the circle broke up, their faces were strained.

"Ah, so what's the verdict?" Jessica asked. "Do you like your quarters?"

"The room is wonderful. I have to tell you, though, its shape makes me feel like a small marble rattling about in a giant cylinder." Sari added, "That's a joke. Really, Jessica, the room is out of this world."

"My wife wanted to put you in another one, nearer to the rest of us, but the tower was how the Duchess planned it," Monty said.

"And what the Duchess says, goes." Jessica's stiff smile did not mask her irritation. "I told her I felt you'd be happier elsewhere, because that tower...well, remember all those queens and other dissidents who were banished to a tower, then dragged out and beheaded? To my way of thinking, it's just too gruesome."

Sari tried to read her expression but failed. "Come on, Jessica," she blurted, "this is the twentieth century, and I'm a sound sleeper, not given to nightmares. Not yet, anyway. So please don't worry about me."

"If you say so."

From beneath heavy brows, Monty frowned and changed the subject. "Shall we eat?"

"Good idea. Let's sit down," Jessica said. "I'm sure our guests are starving."

It amused Sari to watch the chauffeur and the "unofficial housekeeper"—members of the castle staff—seating themselves at either end of the table. They were acting just like the lord and lady of the castle. Then she understood. Or she thought she did.

From all that Marianne had said, she surmised that her grandmother was absent much of the time, jetting to one spa or another, from this continent to that, then off to visit her villa on the Amalfi Coast or her chalet in Switzerland. So Jessica naturally filled in for her as presiding hostess.

And it became clear as the meal progressed that she had developed into a fine one. She had unflappable poise as she kept the traffic moving smoothly in and out of the kitchen. But Jessica's nervousness was apparent as her hands twisted and untwisted the chain that held her locket. If she were aware of her mood, she made no effort to lighten up.

Oscar Drayton, Esq., was also decidedly ill at ease. Rotund as one of those jumbo balloons used as punching bags by children, he seemed to be slowly shrinking. Sari knew it was only an optical illusion, yet his chins sagged and that generous mouth, made for smiling, pouted at the corners. Like Monty, he was not eating, only fiddling with his knife and fork and pushing the food around on his plate. Oscar had evidently been thrown by the Duchess' untimely disappearance.

Or did her attorney know more than he was telling?

And Ron. It was apparent that he had decided to try to impress Sari, his new audience. Even if no one else laughed at his jokes or listened to his tales of narrow escapes on the highway, she seemed attentive.

"I'm at the place now," he said, "where I can pass up hauling a load if I feel like going in a different direction." He favored Sari with another low whistle. "Or if some gal gives me a tumble."

Despite his brashness and unceasing flattery, Sari was beginning to look more kindly on this man who preened himself without lifting a finger. She had to respect his willingness to manufacture small talk in order to keep a dull dinner party from expiring.

Sari knew that in his search for a topic he would eventually get around to commenting on her name. Most people were curious about it. "Sari. Now, that's a new one. I bet you wish you had a buck for every time you've been asked where you got your name. It has an oriental ring to it. By any chance, is it Indian?"

She was pleased. "Very good, Ron. It's what the dress worn by Indian ladies is called. My mother was a missionary who had real love for the women she served. She'd do anything to get close to them. She adopted the native mode of dress, and even wore her hair long and loose and parted in the middle like theirs."

Sari sighed. "Mom looked just like the other ladies, with her sari wrapped about her with one end over her head to protect her from the hot sun. It was so like her to think the word Sari had a nice sound." She spread her hands. "And that's how I got my unusual name."

"It suits you, it really does. I like it."

"I got my first sari for my tenth birthday. It was beautiful, and my mom made it herself. It was the last present she gave me before she passed away."

To her surprise, Sari wished Ron could have seen them in their saris with their hair—Mother's jet black and her red hair—brushed until it shone, and Daddy looking on proudly as the birthday girl blew out the ten candles on the chewy raisin-spice cake.

That meal had been specially festive. If Sari closed her eyelids, she could still smell the pungent aroma of curry that had pervaded the love-filled cottage where God had always seemed so close—so different from the way things were with her now. God had become a stranger. And she was here in another time, another place, where the air crackled with tension.

Chapter Five

The heavy chair toppled under her as Sari rose abruptly. "Will you all excuse me? I really am awfully tired." And she bolted.

"Wait!" Jessica called. "Are you sure you can find your way?"

By the time Jessica caught up with her, Sari had herself under control. "A touch of homesickness?" the housekeeper asked kindly. "Well, Sari, whether you miss India or Manhattan makes no difference—any place would be preferable to this stupid hunk of rock. Anyway, I thought I'd better tell you the matches are in the desk, in case you want to use the heater."

"When it's so warm?"

"We do happen to be well over five thousand feet altitude. The castle is poorly insulated and from the middle of August it tends to get chilly before morning." Scornfully, the housekeeper repeated, "Stupid old castle."

Jessica tossed her curls as she turned to rejoin the others for after-dinner coffee, leaving Sari with the impression that Monty and his wife appeared to be exact opposites in temperament, especially in the way they viewed the castle. Even through Monty's aloofness, Sari could sense the pride that was apparent at the mere mention of this structure that looked as if it had sprung from the dusty Arizona soil. It was obvious he loved every square inch of Hudspith Castle. And why shouldn't he, since he was British to the core?

On the other hand, his wife's roots were in the West. Her natural habitat most likely would be a nice tri-level or spacious ranch-style home in a friendly neighborhood—quite different from life in a castle. Jessica could do without the corps of servants and the pomp and ceremony for which Monty hankered.

The climate around the table had been so disquieting that Sari did not mind the sepulchral silence as she hurried through the hallways toward her room in the tower that was, as she had been warned, extremely isolated.

In her absence, the bed covers had been turned down and her gown laid out. She undressed and used the small step stool to climb into the four-poster. She stretched luxuriously. What a fantastic room, and it was hers for the moment, courtesy of the grandmother who, for some unfathomable reason, had finally decided to recognize their blood tie.

But why now? Where had she been in Sari's time of crisis eight years ago? Where was she when Sari needed her? What was behind this belated desire to make contact?

The very phrasing of the telegram she had received at her apartment yesterday still infuriated Sari: "Your grandmother is waiting to see you...it is hoped you will drop everything...she will expect you...come to Arizona."

She had bristled as she read and reread the words. She was already twenty-four. After all the lost years, how could this cold aloof grandparent "expect" her to do anything or go anywhere? What right did she have to dictate?

As she settled against down-filled pillows in her grandmother's canopied featherbed, Sari decided she'd most certainly turn this visit to her own advantage.

"I'm going to ask her if she ever wondered about her son's life on the other side of the world," Sari told herself. "Will her lips curl in distaste when I tell her about the kind of food he had to eat? And the drafty dirt-floored cottage he lived in?"

Its image was as clear in Sari's mind as though she had been away from that humble dwelling only a few days. Constructed of mud bricks plastered together with river clay, their cottage had looked just like all the others in the crowded dusty town on the edge of India. But there was one great difference—its open door was always bulging with sick and seeking villagers. Sari's missionary parents were angels of mercy and, as they moved among the needy people, their love and compassion had spilled over onto all of them.

The natives had become their family while Sari's mother and father found the grace to live with the rejection meted out by his mother. Nevertheless, they could not completely hide their sorrow at the lack of communication with their only living relative. Often, late at night, Sari would hear her mother weeping and she would hide her head under the sheet to shut out the sound of her father's heavy sighs.

Sari did not fully understand the extent of their suffering until India's torrid climate claimed the life of her mother. She craved—and needed—the precious relationship and security a caring grandma could have supplied. The sense of abandonment cut deeply. In her heart the root of bitterness burrowed deeper and began to flourish.

A half dozen years later, when Sari was sixteen, her father fell ill with fever. As she pressed the cool compresses on his head, she begged him to allow her to write to her grandmother.

"Daddy, your medicines are so expensive!" she cried. "She can easily spare the money for your prescriptions. And just think, Daddy, if she came through, we could go up into the hills where it's not so hot. Under those cool trees you'd be well in no time. Let's write to her."

"My poor baby, how can I make you understand? A long time ago your grandmother made it very clear that she was washing her hands of me. The last thing I'll ever do is ask her for financial help. Try not to worry your sweet head about anything. We'll make out all right."

She stared at him in bewilderment. "But she's your mom. She ought to care about us."

"Our God has never forgotten us, has He? He'll continue to take care of us now."

Sari felt like stamping her foot. "I hate her. Do you hear me? I hate her!"

Weakly, he stroked Sari's hair. "My darling, do you know how I've always thought of you? You've been just like a candle shining with faith and love that has brightened this dark corner of the world for me. Please don't let that brave little flame be snuffed out by hard feelings. Keep on shining, sweetheart."

With the help of an itinerant missionary doctor, she managed to nurse her father back to a fragile measure of health, but it soon became apparent that the rigors of pioneer missionary work had exacted their toll. Her father's usefulness on the continent was ended, and Mission Headquarters informed them that he was to be sent home.

Sari had not been surprised that upon hearing the news he snapped his fingers and exclaimed, "This isn't the end of the world, you know. In fact, we'll make it an exciting adventure." She stared at him. It was exactly the sort of perky reaction she would have expected from the one who had always managed to hang onto his optimistic attitude toward life, even in the face of repudiation and betrayal.

"What do you mean? What kind of adventure?"

"Do you remember how I told you about your mama coming from Canada as a single worker to the field and that she had spent a week in New York City on the way? I can still hear her saying she felt she hadn't really lived before she saw Manhattan. Well, little girl," he announced, "I'm going to ask the board to send us to New York. I think it will be great fun to live there. Shall we do it?"

"Oh, yes!"

His request was granted and within a few weeks they were settled in a small midtown flat. Their life seemed to have taken a turn for the better. Sari was delighted that her father's color was returning as they did all the things her mother had talked about: The Staten Island Ferry, Empire State Building, Bronx Zoo. They spent hours riding what she had called "the tube."

As the weeks sped by, her father began to talk about returning to his beloved adopted land; however, it was not to be. He collapsed once more.

As Sari watched their meager funds dwindle and listened to his shallow breathing, she worried about how they were going to survive. She thought again of the grandmother who had written them off. Granted, she was an insulated creature with a heart of ice, but surely she would feel a scrap of pity and come to their rescue.

"Daddy," she had pleaded, "can't we contact Grandma?"

He shook his head. "I am so sorry, sweetheart, that things haven't been different. I can't expect you to understand. Please, just forgive me, but I can't intrude on her life."

"All right, Daddy," she told him. And added silently, "You can't, but I can."

While her father napped, Sari had gone through his private papers looking for her grandmother's address.

She knew he had always devoured every word in *The Guardian* sent to him from a colleague in London. By means of the society pages, he had kept track of his mother and her activities. He even knew when she had remarried. Sari was sure her address was somewhere in his records. She went through everything twice, then burst into tears when she came up empty-handed.

As a last resort, she had written to the Mission Board. If anybody could help her locate her grandmother, they could. To her relief, the answer came back from London in record time.

Her mouth fell open as she pulled the letter from the envelope. The news it contained was so amazing that she had to read it twice to make sure she understood. Her father's mother didn't live in England. Apparently, she had relocated in Arizona.

Sari gasped at the thought that her grandmother was here in the same country, just a couple thousand miles away. She could hop on a transcontinental flight and be at her son's bedside in a flash.

Sari had scribbled an urgent appeal that went out that same afternoon to the post office box number in Prescott. As she visualized the joyful reunion that was sure to take place, she felt like hugging herself. It won't be long now, she thought. Daddy will forgive me for going against his wishes because just seeing his mother will be like a dose of miracle medicine.

As the weeks passed, however, Sari realized she had wasted the stamp. There was no reply. Her plea had fallen on deliberately-deafened ears. Her grandmother was not going to blast into nothingness the barrier she'd erected between herself and her own flesh and blood. The woman was apparently so stubborn that she would never budge.

For Sari, it was the last straw.

She had been the solitary mourner at her father's burial and while she stood beside the newly-filled grave, she had made a solemn vow to herself. One day, when she finally met her grandmother, she would make her admit her cruelty. Sari would watch her grovel and ask for forgiveness. The woman had consigned her own son to never-never land, and sooner or later the day of reckoning would arrive.

Thanks to her grandmother's imperious order, that day had now come. It was a self-satisfying thought as Sari lay back in the featherbed. She felt herself begin to unwind, drifting over the edge into sleep. Suddenly, a ghostly elusive whispering pulled her back to reality. Sari strained to hear the garbled murmur. Where was the whispering coming from?

With a shudder she told herself to stop being silly and go to sleep. Vague noises were always part of a castle's mystique. She began to breathe easier, but the persistent whispering continued. It made her skin crawl. Impossible though it seemed, the sound seemed to be coming from the stone wall behind the bed.

Abruptly, the mystery was compounded by the grating of the door handle. Sari jerked upright and stared at the knob. Was she imagining it was moving?

To her relief, the rattling ceased as suddenly as it had begun. Even though she knew they would say she was just being squeamish, she considered joining the others in the east wing, which might as well have been on the moon because she still didn't have her bearings.

Even the sight of Monty with his moody, ambivalent nature would be welcome now, and the thought of his wife even more comforting. Jessica seemed so down to earth. Dependable.

Then there was Oscar Drayton. Sari's first impression of her grandmother's attorney had been that here was a well-nourished individual who covered his real feelings with the sort of carefree mask affected by many overweight people. But Oscar would be a good man to have around in an emergency.

And finally, suave Ron Cooper. She was frightened enough to brave his scorn. She backed down, however, after she cracked the door and peeked out.

In the halfhearted glow of intermittent pools of light, the corridor stretched forever. Sari had to admit she was not up to facing the deserted, echoing hallways. Not when she was ready to jump at her own shadow.

Quickly, she retreated. "Too bad I don't have the long security bar from my Manhattan apartment," she muttered as she dragged the plump armchair across the room. After she braced it under the doorknob, she crawled back in bed and pulled the covers up to her neck.

Squealing radiator pipes, busy elevators grinding, ambulance sirens—these she understood. She was not used to being frightened by disembodied noises she could not identify. It was too-eerie a climax to a perplexing day; a day, she soon discovered, that was not quite over.

As she tried to relax, Sari felt her stomach suddenly twist into a tight nervous knot when the secretive mumbling picked up once more. And was she hearing her own name? "Sari...Sari."

Shivering, she stood on the bed, reached behind her, and rubbed her hand on the bumpy wall. She laughed uneasily. "Stones don't talk!" she declared loudly. She was perfectly safe here in this fantastic tower room. There was nothing to be afraid of, was there?

As she punched the pillow, she was sure she would never get to sleep. And her last thought before slumber finally claimed her was that somebody was going to hear what she thought about her first wretched night in Hudspith Castle.

That person turned out to be Oscar Drayton.

Chapter Six

The next morning Sari found the lawyer on the garden terrace. Dapper in a bright green and white checked jacket, he was serving himself from the breakfast buffet. When Sari joined him at one of the glass-topped tables, his smile turned to a frown and he asked, "Oh my, didn't you sleep well?"

"No. In fact, I slept very little. Mr. Drayton, what would you say if I told you someone was creeping around in the hall outside my room last night?"

"Sari, I'm 'Oscar' to my friends." He smiled. "My dear, I felt that what was said at the dinner table—references to incarcerated queens and such nonsense—was in poor taste. After all, you were lodged in a tower and of course your imagination was kindled. However, this is the new world and this is a civilized castle."

Though he covered his mouth with his napkin, he was unable to hide his amusement. Sari frowned. "I mean it. I heard someone."

"Have you considered it may have been nothing but a practical joke, capitalizing on the traditional spookiness associated with a place such as this one? I hear you know a great deal about castles, so you know what I'm talking about. I do hope you don't begin to build portents of evil into ordinary sounds. Hudspith Castle is full of sounds."

"I'm not making this up!"

"I think you should just chalk up the experience to the power of suggestion or flight fatigue and put it out of your mind. When you start seeing some of these mystifications, that will be the time to worry. We'll all be in trouble then."

As Oscar gave his attention to the toast he was buttering, Sari was glad to see a twinkle in his eyes. He had recovered his ebullient spirit. This seemed more like the real Oscar Drayton; the one at dinner last night had been a troubled man.

"Your visit to Hudspith Castle should be one of the highlights of your life," he reminded her. "It's a shame you have gotten off on the wrong foot."

She wondered what he would say if she told him about the whispers. But as she sat there on the sunlit terrace, feeling relaxed and confident, Sari was tempted to think she really hadn't heard the whispers. She asked Oscar about her grandmother's motives in summoning her.

"I assume you know of the rift between her and my dad. She never wanted to have anything to do with me, either, and I mean never. So why now?"

"I'm not sure. Perhaps she just wants to get acquainted. Better late than never, you know."

"Oscar, I feel as though I'm in limbo. It doesn't seem right to even enjoy this food when we don't know where she is. And, talking about whereabouts—I've moved half a dozen times since Dad and I left India and settled in New York, so how did she track me down?"

"Believe me, Sari, for anyone with sufficient capital, there's nothing that can't be uncovered. She simply asked me to hire experts, and they worked fast. In less than two days they had completed the job. Naturally, that sort of digging is expensive, but she made it plain that cost was no object."

"And I'll bet she's accustomed to getting what she wants," Sari commented. "Tell me more about her."

She planted her chin on her hands and waited while Oscar helped himself to marmalade. Once he started talking, he warmed to his subject. "She's looked upon as an important person in Southwestern society, and she's an avid philanthropist when it comes to benefits, fund-raising and such.

"She sponsors a lot of fund-raising events right here in the castle, for charity and causes she believes in, such as wiping out substance abuse. Her favorite, though, seems to be the highly-popular "Up With Families," which is women banding together to strengthen the family unit. A most rewarding sort of life, don't you agree?"

"Well, of course." Sari stared at Oscar as she absorbed this new revelation. My grandmother is gung ho for familial togetherness? That's a laugh, she thought.

"She outlived two spouses," Oscar continued. "Your Grandpa Geoffrey was one of those lucky people who was born with a silver spoon in his mouth, and he used it to scoop up a mega-fortune, which he left to his wife. It must be true, though, that money can't buy happiness. I don't think that was one of those marriages you hear about that are made in heaven. I suspect no one would've been greatly surprised to see her remain a widow. But she was swept off her feet by a gallant Welshman."

"The Duke."

"Right. At first glance, they were a most unlikely match. Oliver, the Duke of Rhysbury, would have described his own family as 'upper crust but bloody poor' which, translated into Americanese means 'genteel but impoverished nobility.' He was a very talented gentleman, though. Drawing on his wife's bottomless funds, he accomplished the stupendous feat of replicating this castle when they decided to move to this country and to the state she'd fallen in love with. Actually, I think Ollie kept her laughing with his often-zany ideas. He was a delightful Welsh Walt Disney, a child at heart."

The lawyer looked at his watch, but Sari had not finished with her questions. "Oscar," she persisted, "what is she really like? Can you describe her personality?"

Sari did not understand the irresistible curiosity she was feeling. It was almost as though the Duchess was not her grandmother, but an intriguing individual about whom she wanted to learn more. Sari already knew she was a benevolent do-gooder. All of this, yet with a heart of stone where her own kinfolk were concerned. She was a puzzle. And Sari felt the drive to solve the mystery surrounding her.

Chuckling, Oscar reached for a banana. As he peeled it, he said, "Sari, I don't know anyone else who is quite like her. Unlike some seniors, she hasn't become a recluse. With each passing year she seems to grow younger. Besides travel outside the country, she makes frequent trips to visit her doctor in Los Angeles and to meet her friends in Phoenix and Tucson. And Palm Springs, where she golfs."

Sari pressed for more details. "So she isn't frail?"

He smiled. "If you mean, is she ready for that ol' rocking chair? Definitely not! She is about your size, five feet four or so, and she keeps fit. She's never slow to tackle something new, like the exercising equipment coming out nowadays. She's game for anything, like learning how to play chess. Ollie was a master at it, and they played regularly together in that marvelous gazebo until the day he died."

"You make her sound so 'with it' and so organized. Yet sending for me sounds like a spur of the moment thing."

"I agree with you. I didn't hear about it until she

called me from L.A. on Saturday. I carried out her instructions, and now you are here."

"And she isn't! Oscar, does just taking off without saying where she'll be seem sensible to you?"

"Well, I've known her for years and she sets her own agenda. On Monday everything seemed to have been normal. Piloting her little Cessna, she left LAX about four o'clock, landed at Prescott, jumped into her car and tootled on home. She met with her staff. From what Jessica reports, it wasn't so much what she said, as what she didn't say, but change was in the air and people could feel it. According to Jessica, the Duchess was excited and very 'up.'"

"I hate for this to sound like a third degree, but what do you think happened? Where do you think she went?"

"You've got me there. However, I tend to subscribe to the opinion expressed by Jessica: the Duchess will be back when she's good and ready and not a second before."

Sari was listening to Oscar's tone of voice. He was much too blasé. He might have been discussing something as mundane as misplacing an outdated law book.

She studied him through narrowed lids. He was so disturbed last night, but you wouldn't know it by listening to him now.

Oscar, in turn, was studying Sari. His whole body seemed to have stopped moving, chewing, and breathing. He was watching her the same way a spider watches a fly who is teetering on the perimeter of the web.

She got up. "Thanks for your time, Oscar."

Looking back from inside the great hall, she saw that he still held that stiff, poised position, only now his round head was cocked to one side of his heavy neck. The events of the previous evening flashed across Sari's mind. She suspected that Oscar Drayton knew more than he was letting on.

When Sari reached the front door, she ran into Ron

Cooper on the steps. He was dressed in tennis shorts and carried a racket. His eyes lit up when he saw her. "I'm on my way to the court. I can get you a racket. How about a game?"

"Sorry, I don't play. Who's your usual partner?"

"There's this guy who was into tournaments—at Wimbledon, no less—and he enjoys a few sets once in awhile, like when I come up. He's great with animals. They're his first love. Pete is in charge of the Duchess' stables."

"Really? I love horses," Sari said. "Needless to say, I didn't have much opportunity to ride horses in New York City. But jogging," she added, "that's something else. Michael and I used to run just about every morning from my apartment building down Riverside Drive."

"Hmm. Michael, huh? So tell me, who's Michael?"

She swallowed hard. "Nobody special, just a man I knew in Manhattan."

"Knew. Is that past tense?"

"You could say that." She nodded vigorously. "Yes, past tense."

"All right!" Taking her hand, he led her down the stairs, over the cobblestones, past the pool and up a curving rise to what appeared at first glance to be a collection of tall, chunky, oddly-shaped objects. "How does a round of golf grab you, m'lady? The Duke pulled out all the stops on this little project."

"Miniature golf? I love it!" She was enchanted as her companion produced the necessary implements, and they began to play.

She soon discovered that this course was flagrantly British. The first challenge she faced was Westminster Abbey, where the ball was propelled through an archway without, so she hoped, clobbering the bridal pair just emerging. Next came Big Ben and a wicked-looking pendulum erratically swinging back and forth.

She giggled at a chocolate brown horse whose hooves

moved so rapidly that her ball barely skimmed past. If she hadn't been successful, the Buckingham Palace guard was ready to brandish a sword that would have been certain to knock the white pill into the rough. And these were the easy holes.

At the sixth they rested under a cottonwood tree while Sari tried to recover her self-confidence after fishing her ball out of the River Thames for the eighth time. She turned to Ron and broached the subject that was foremost on her mind.

"Can we talk about my grandmother?" she began. "The way I look at it, there are two possible reasons for her absence. Number one, she had overlooked some prior commitment, and she phoned a friend to pick her up on the road. Or, two, she's been kidnapped."

"Aha! So that's what you are—a detective disguised as a delectable redhead. Sure, she might have called someone. She's got lots of friends, and she may have decided to stay over. For all she knew, you were still on the East Coast, and it wouldn't matter if she weren't here."

"And the other? It happens all the time to wealthy people."

"In New York."

"Here in Arizona, too."

"Sari, it's a bit premature to be talking about body-snatching."

"I don't think it's such a far-out idea," she retorted, "and I believe we ought to do something positive. Listen. I met a very nice lady on the plane, one of my grandmother's acquaintances who lives in Prescott. She said if I needed anything, to get in touch. I'll call and ask if she's seen her."

Ron shook his head. "Do you want her to go to the police? Have you forgotten that kidnapping last year, the one where the family dashed right out to blab the news? If they'd waited, the victim might have been released unharmed. As it was, some kids found his body in a ditch three weeks later."

Sari did remember the case and shuddered. The story had been splashed across the tabloids and the family was harshly criticized. They could not be patient. They couldn't wait to be notified by those who committed the crime.

Ron looked so serious that Sari conceded, "You're probably right. After all, not even twenty-four hours have passed, and I guess I'm being too melodramatic. I'll have to hold onto the hope that she's sitting someplace right now, sipping tea and as right as rain."

"Now you're being smart."

"The flip side of all this is, the longer my grandmother stays away, the more exploring I can get done. You know, peeking behind all those mysterious closed doors, hidden passageways, all that kind of thing."

Sari was surprised at Ron's heavy response to her remark. The golden sparks in his eyes flickered for only an instant before his lashes veiled them. He looked just as Oscar Drayton had when she left him on the terrace. Ron sat still as a statue, barely breathing.

"Why the funny mood, Ron?"

He lifted a shoulder. "Not a thing, my love. But are you forgetting that castles can be overwhelming? This one is no exception."

"Don't tell me you're afraid I might accidentally lock myself in a secret dungeon."

"No, that happens only in fairy tales." He handed Sari her club. "Now, how about wrapping up this golf game?"

At the ninth hole, she had to gauge the rising curtain and sail the ball into Judy's hands before Punch's fist swiveled around to send it into the rough.

"Hole in one!" Ron grinned. "Ollie would have been proud of you."

"Thanks. And now I'm on my way to explore the

unknown territory inside the castle," Sari announced. "I plan to start out at the end of the east wing and work my way through the kitchens and pantries around to the front, then back to the opposite end. After that, I'll explore the upstairs." Sari clasped her hands and sighed contentedly, "What a treat!"

"I'll tag along."

"Not a chance, Ron."

"Please. You've no idea of how vast this place is."

"I know. That's part of its appeal." Sari had not forgotten that he had accused her of being the kind of female who is leery of her own shadow. Well, she would show him. "Ron, do you really think I'd let you spoil my fun? See you later."

Had those been alarm signals that deepened the yellow irises in Ron's eyes or was he just being his flirting, affable self? Either way, Sari was glad she hadn't told him about last night's nerve-racking experience. Then, Ron certainly wouldn't have taken "no" for an answer. He would have insisted on going with her. But this was the sort of adventure she wanted to enjoy on her own.

Chapter Seven

Sari soon found that the adjective Ron had used was apropos: the castle was vast. There were too many rooms to count. In contrast to the dim corridors, the rooms were light and airy. There were bowls of fresh flowers everywhere.

Hallways branched off other hallways, short flights of steps appeared where least expected, and passages were curved. It was complicated and confusing and exactly how Sari would have expected a castle, facsimile notwithstanding, to be.

She had assumed that all the usual references to creaking floor boards, squeaking door hinges, and shifting shadows were only fiction dreamed up by authors to add spice to their tales of suspense. By the time she reached the second floor, however, she was sure they had to have gleaned their knowledge right on the spot by spending time in a castle such as this one.

Sari had lost all track of time when it dawned on her that the sounds she was hearing were the footsteps of someone pacing behind her. Such sounds were not new to her; she had heard them on the streets of Manhattan—careful, measured footfalls unlike those of a person on legitimate business.

Why would anyone want to follow her? Holding her breath, she whipped around. Even though there was nobody there in the pale emptiness, she panicked and was immediately adrift in unfamiliar surroundings.

As Sari raced down a curved corridor, she wished she had not been so adamant with Ron Cooper. But it was too late to be sorry now. She had gotten what she asked for, a chance to be alone. Alone with the eerie sound of footsteps closing in behind her.

Gasping, she saw what appeared to be an open doorway. She sprinted toward it. It was only a little farther. Just then, Ron stepped out in front of her and, with a choking sob, Sari fell into his arms.

Smiling broadly, he held her close while he pulled out a handkerchief and gently blotted her cheeks. "Hey, this is unexpected. And to what do I owe the pleasure of your company?" She clung to him as he stroked her hair and whispered, "Those are real tears. Why are you crying?"

"Somebody was following me. It was terrible! Ron, you should have heard the footsteps."

"Sweetheart, there are plenty of people moving about in this castle. I doubt anyone has time for such games."

"It wasn't a game!"

Behind her she saw a man emerging from the shadows. He sounded out of breath as he asked, "Ron, is she all right? Is Sari okay?"

Her heart nearly turned over as her brain registered the fact that it was Monty. Was he the one who had been stalking her?

Ron's lips brushed her forehead. "Mont, it seems Sari has caught castle fever. She hears noises when she ought to be sleeping and, as if that weren't bad enough, she hears them in the daytime, too. Right, honey?"

His bantering brought Sari to her senses. "Oscar told

you about last night. And you don't believe me, either. Fine! Why should I try to convince you someone was following me just now?"

Over Ron's shoulder she saw the glittering chandelier suspended over the great hall and knew where she was. Glaring at Ron, she pushed herself away from his chest, cast a withering glance at the chauffeur and turned on her heel.

At the front of the gallery, Sari encountered Marianne who clucked like a mother hen and rushed to put a steadying arm about her. "You're white as a sheet. You look as if you're going to keel over. What happened?"

The maid's concern set Sari to crying again. "I-I-I got lost, that's all."

"I'm relieved. From the look of you, I thought it was something dreadful."

If Marianne only knew, Sari thought. It is dreadful. Twelve hours ago I was scared out of my wits and now this. Are the two events related? Was the chauffeur involved both times?

The implications of this possibility kept Sari silent as Marianne led her to the tower where, too weak to object, she agreed to lie down on the chaise.

"We have to get some color back into your cheeks," Marianne said. "I think you should rest until lunchtime."

"Lunch?" She couldn't face Monty. "No," Sari said, "I don't think I can swallow a bite. I'll skip lunch."

"That's what the Duchess always says. But she changes her mind and you will, too, when I fix one of my nice trays and bring it up to you." The maid paused, then added, "Is there more to it than just losing your way? Do you want to tell me about it? Besides making you feel better, I may be able to help."

"I'm not sure. Yes, maybe you can. Marianne, tell me who might follow me, furtively, through the corridors. It sounds absurd but it's true. Someone did just that."

"That's vicious!" Marianne's eyes widened. "Frankly, I can't think who would stoop to do such a thing. And for what purpose? Shall I speak to Monty about it?"

"No! Please don't mention it to him."

Marianne opened her mouth but apparently thought better of what she had been about to say. "Very well." She covered Sari with an afghan. "I'll pop on down to the kitchen. Be back in a jiffy."

Closing her eyes, Sari relived the desperate moments just before she reached the safe haven of Ron's strong arms. She squirmed as she remembered his kiss on her temple and how she had felt when he poked fun at her and put her down. Even though she knew it was all in fun, it hurt. It hurt a lot, the way it does when you care about someone.

Shocked, Sari asked, What are you thinking, girl? Ron isn't your kind of man. Forget him.

Determined not to acknowledge the undesirable, growing attraction she was beginning to feel toward Ron, Sari pressed her face into the cushions and did her best to put him out of her mind. She dozed off and, in her uneasy dreams, she could not escape as Ron chased her up the green fairways on the miniature golf course and over the comical traps. She looked back at him and his arms were stretched out to catch her when she fell over the side.

"Here we are," Marianne's cheerful voice scattered the dream. "And doesn't this look good enough to eat?"

Depositing a tray on the chocolate table, she propped Sari up with pillows, then opened a napkin and laid it across her lap. "We call this the Ploughman's lunch. It's a favorite not only out in the fields but in every pub all over the English countryside. See, you have a delicious crusty roll, tomato and lettuce, and a wedge of Cheddar cheese. Plus pickled onions. The Duchess likes this repast because it's so low in calories."

"Not a bad idea, seeing the way I've been stuffing

myself ever since I hit Arizona. But," Sari raised an eyebrow, "where does that yummy strawberry tart fit in?"

Marianne grinned. "It's mostly fruit. Now, you tuck into this and you'll be feeling fit again. Sari, would you mind if I stay while you're eating? Ever since the Duchess told us you were coming and I knew you had grown up on the mission field, I could hardly wait to meet you. I can't tell you what it means to know you're a Christian."

When Sari made no response, the maid continued, "I even had this wild notion—maybe you would consent to do some Bible study with me. I'm sure there's a lot that you could teach me. The Lord Jesus is my all in all, and it hasn't been easy to live among those who have no time for God. Especially your grandma."

The cornflower blue eyes filled with tears. "I'm sure you realize how very much she needs Him. I've been praising the Lord for you, Sari, and I'm so glad you're here. The prayers of one believer are good, but the intercession of two believers is even better, so I thought we might make a pact to earnestly pray for your grandmother. Is it a deal?"

While Marianne waited for an answer, Sari stared at a loose thread in the afghan, smoothing it with a fingernail while she debated with herself. So this was why this particular girl had sought her out. It wasn't because time hung heavy on her hands or that she was looking for odd jobs to fill it. Marianne thought that Sari was a kindred spirit.

Sari wondered if the maid would still want to be her friend if she told her the real reason she was here. Even worse, if she confessed the hatred that had spread within her like some malignant growth, would Marianne be so turned off that she wouldn't speak to her again?

Sari stopped debating with herself and did the only thing she could do. "Well, sure," she stammered hoarsely. She liked Marianne and she did not want to jeopardize her new friendship with this sweet English lady. But this was a promise she had no intention of keeping. Nothing in Sari's expression revealed the sour thoughts she harbored. Pray for her grandmother? That was the last thing she'd ever do.

Marianne beamed, apparently satisfied they were on the same spiritual wavelength. "This is a lovely day," she said, "so what have you planned for this afternoon?"

"It's pretty fanciful, but I've been thinking about the carved railings and broad merlons on top of this round tower. It's sort of like an exciting Christmas present, the one left under the tree until all the others have been opened. Marianne, I want to climb to the roof—to the rampart. Though it probably sounds trite, I'd like to stand up there and look out over the parapet and feel like the queen of all I survey. For once in my life!"

Sari had suspected the English girl would be empathetic toward her sentiments, and she was not disappointed in the maid's reaction. "My, yes!" Marianne agreed. "To have the breeze blowing in your face and a marvelous view spread before you—mountain peaks, giant trees, Arizona's sapphire sky and fluffy cloud formations. Sorry; I sound like the Chamber of Commerce, don't I?"

Then she shook her head. "But Sari, you can't do that. There is no way. Remember, the floor above is not in use. The steps from the gallery are bricked up."

"Then I'll have to find another way, even if it means climbing to the parapet on a rope from my balcony. Marianne, I've never been more serious."

"May I speak bluntly? Please, Sari, do not pursue this."

"No offense, but I'll find out how Jessica feels about it."

"I already know what she will say. There are so many

other activities here at Hudspith Castle that are safe. It will be best to just forget about the tower roof," Marianne said.

Sari didn't know how to answer her. The change in the tone of the soft voice was so abrupt and laced with fear that it startled her. And why had Marianne's amiable countenance taken on a shuttered look?

As soon as the maid collected the tray and left, Sari threw aside the afghan. She hadn't forgotten what Marianne had said about the "lovely day." She decided to go outside and enjoy it. She slipped into a pair of jeans and her coolest blouse. Then, picking up a magazine, she hurried downstairs and turned toward the garden.

As she approached the summerhouse, the sight of the burnished eagle floating above it caused her to pause. With the sun setting its wings afire and lighting the haughty gleam in its cobalt eyes, the eagle was the sort of showy unconventionality she had begun to expect here. It may have been placed on top of the gazebo in some flight of creative fancy, but the warlike regal bird with spreading talons made a most prestigious weather vane.

Inside, the lattice-framed summerhouse lived up to its promise. It was a restful bower with comfortable cretonne-covered benches and an octagonal table that held the chief attraction. This was a sleek, inlaid marble-topped playing board with a set of markers carved from desert rock waiting on its satiny surface.

Everything was in place, ready for the moment when someone would begin moving, eliminating, checkmating. Sari picked up several of the pieces and hefted them appreciatively. Her knowledge of the game was nil, but Ollie's chess board certainly was a nice touch.

Her gaze traveled over the garden as she admired the beds of zinnias and snapdragons, prickly cactus plants in rock plots, and thick bushes snuggled against the castle walls behind a profusion of blooming sweet peas.

Trimmed hedges enclosed carefully-raked dirt paths that crisscrossed the wide expanse. She sat in perfumed seclusion, screened in by rambler roses. She felt a welcome sense of well-being.

As she enjoyed the solitude, that unsettling, nagging preoccupation with her grandmother returned. Her "missing" grandmother. "Missing. What a dismal word that is," she whispered. It made her shudder, as though a raw wind had just blown down from the heights of Spruce Mountain.

The cozy gazebo suddenly became an alien place. Sari closed her magazine and sprang to her feet. Walking rapidly, she rounded the east wing and came to a footpath leading downward at right angles. She had no idea where she was going; she only knew she had to distance herself from the summerhouse.

True to Monty's description of this side of the property, here was the precipitous embankment artistically landscaped in a series of terraces with hedges and baby palms. Farther on, Sari saw a group of squat adobe dwellings with red tile roofs. Spaced out behind log fences, they were rustic, yet attractive cabins one would expect to find on a Western ranch.

Sari was calmed by the sight that seemed a world removed from Hudspith Castle and its medieval atmosphere—until she made the mistake of looking over her shoulder. She saw the chauffeur polishing the Rolls Royce in front of the large garage. The memory of her flight through castle halls set her heart to pounding as she scurried toward the cabins.

She had never been close to a bunkhouse before. There was something halcyon about the scene that included rocking chairs swaying on the porches and window boxes filled with red and orange geraniums. Her breathing steadied. When she noticed the door of the last house was ajar, she couldn't resist going up the steps and peering inside.

This was unmistakably a man's abode. But curtains bright with colorful designs and Navajo rugs covering the plank floor showed that a woman—Jessica, most likely—had had a hand in the decor. The taste in posters and pictures tied in with the cowboy theme, too. But something was missing here. The room was much too neat.

Where was the masculine clutter—scattered newspapers, boots and pants carelessly left where they'd been dropped? Where were the unwashed, messy coffee mugs? The place looked deserted and that meant no one would mind if she examined it more closely.

She crossed toward a Mexican Ojo de Dios hanging on the wall. Then she did a double-take. Oscar Drayton's green and white checked garment was lying, carefully folded, on the table. She turned and smiled as she saw him sprawled in a corner bunk. His feet and a hand, like the appendages of a limp Pillsbury dough boy, dangled over the side. She idly wondered why the attorney would come way out here to a bunkhouse to take a nap.

A moment later, the smile slid off her face. She screamed at the sight of a steady stream of blood that was dripping off his inert fingers onto the floor.

Sari was beside him in an instant. "Oscar! Oscar!" There was no answer. His eyes were closed and there was a ghastly waxen pallor on his normally-ruddy face.

She knew he was dead.

Chapter Eight

Sari was close to fainting as she stumbled blindly through the doorway and down the path. She couldn't get away fast enough from the terrifying sight of Oscar's lifeless form.

In her flight she collided with Monty as he ambled toward her. "Hold on," he said, as he steadied her. "You're trembling. What's the trouble now, dear?"

"It's Oscar. He's dead! Oscar Drayton's dead!"

"I don't believe that's even remotely possible. The little man said he would be in the library working on some papers." Monty's broad grin told Sari what he thought: she was a neurotic female who was seeing things that did not, indeed could not, exist. Again. "I don't want to appear unsympathetic, but go ahead. You have my ear. What's this nonsense about Oscar?"

She hid a stab of anger and shouted, "He's dead! And he's down there in that end cabin."

Monty rolled his eyes and shook his head. "All right. Lead on."

On the porch she stood aside, fighting nausea, bracing herself against the railing as Monty entered and stood studying her grandmother's attorney. He grunted as he leaned over, wrestling with Oscar's bulk and turning him onto his stomach.

A moment later he was pushing her out of the way as he leaped down the stairs. "I'm sorry! You were right on. Oscar's been stabbed, and I've got to get help. He's still breathing, thank God."

Sari's legs had gone all rubbery, and she sank onto the top step with her arms crossed tightly in front of herself to hide her uncontrollable shaking. She looked into the distance, trying vainly to blot out how it had felt to come upon what she had assumed was a dead man. Knowing Oscar was alive did not mean that hideous moment wouldn't stay with her forever.

The question of what he was doing in the bunkhouse crossed her mind again. It seemed a bit far-fetched to think he came out here to meet someone secretly, but what if that were the reason? And who was responsible for wounding him?

When Sari finally saw the chauffeur and Ron running toward her, she scrambled to her feet and watched them bundle Drayton into a blanket.

With Sari bringing up the rear, the two men trundled him as far as the edge of the garden, where they were joined by a couple of ranch hands who helped transfer the lawyer to his room on the castle's second floor.

Their arrival caused a stir and several maids heard the commotion and clustered outside his door. They were quickly dismissed by Jessica. "It's nothing serious, girls. It looks like only a little mishap and nothing to be alarmed about. I'll be asking one or two of you to take turns sitting with our guest, but as for the rest of you, go about your duties, all right?"

"You'll be sending for a doctor, won't you?" Sari asked.

"There's no need for that, is there, Monty?" Ron said. "Won't Jessica be able to do all that should be done?"

"Of course I'm able," she snapped.

Startled by the shrewd, calculating frown on the chauffeur's face, Sari shrank back, recalling the strange light that had flashed from his eyes as he rushed out of the cabin after examining Oscar.

"I don't get it," Sari insisted. "Anyone can see he needs professional attention."

"Sari, it really isn't necessary. Oscar will be in good hands. Besides, when do doctors make house calls?"

"Ron, he's hurt!"

"Just don't you worry." Jessica patted her arm. "Relax. We'll take care of him."

"Aren't you afraid he might die? Ron, I can't believe you're taking this tragedy so lightly."

"Honey," Ron answered her, "it's just a clean, three-inch knife wound in his fat shoulder, and I bet I know how he got it. I bet he stashed his goodies in that bunkhouse and some other guy with a sweet tooth found them. When they mixed it up, our man came out the loser." Leaning over the still form, he sobered. "Monty, I believe the bleeding's stopped. I predict Drayton will make it."

"He jolly well had better." Pulling savagely at his mustache, Monty cast an inscrutable glance at Ron. "Let's get his shirt off; better yet, let's just rip it. He won't be wanting to wear this again, that's for sure."

With delayed reaction, Sari began to shiver. She ran around the gallery and through the maze of corridors until she reached the tower. What kind of people live in this place where you could have a stabbing, yet balk at bringing in medical aid?

Panting, she leaned against her closed door. Why had she permitted herself to be bullied into leaving her New York apartment—that attractive studio that had been vandalized only twice—for this creepy castle and its riddles?

In her present fitful mood, Sari was all too willing to leave her secluded bedroom and join the rest of the party when dinner was announced at eight o'clock. Marianne helped arrange her hair in a French roll with tiny curls at the neck and enthusiastically approved the finishing touch. "I've never seen such an unusual comb," Marianne said. "It's so dainty and old-worldish. Is it an heirloom?"

Sari nodded. "It was my mother's. She took her jewelry case with her when she went to India as a missionary. It was a lovely case made from oyster shells and it was full of stuff—what most people would call pretty trinkets. But, one by one they, as well as the case, were bartered away for things we really needed. Like food! This was the only piece of jewelry left."

"It ties everything together. You're going to be a big hit with Ron Cooper tonight."

Sari frowned. She had not consciously "dressed" with him in mind. She had only hoped it would help take her thoughts off Oscar's distressing plight.

A few moments later when she saw Ron's eyes widen, she remembered Marianne's prediction. With a bow, he tucked her hand under his elbow and escorted her into the dining salon. "Wow! You look wonderful. Sari, have you ever considered modeling as a career? You're wasting your time in an office."

As he held her chair, he noticed her grimace when the sight of Oscar's empty place brought the afternoon's trauma flooding back. He patted her shoulder. "I know. Our group of five has dwindled to four. But, thanks to your investigative nature, Oscar didn't bleed to death. He's still numbered among the living. Jessica's got him sedated, and he's resting as comfortably as can be expected. Now that's a good reason to put on your happy face, right? So let's see that smile of yours."

Leaning close, he whispered, "You're dazzling tonight. I'll bet that outfit is one of those saris you mentioned. It looks like the real McCoy."

"Not exactly; it's just the way the material is draped

over this white bodice that fools you. There are yards of material in a genuine sari, and they're long enough to touch the floor."

It was all she could do to keep from covering her cheeks with her hands. They burned with memories of the snowy afternoon she and Michael had spent browsing in a colorful boutique in Greenwich Village where he had spotted the lacy, emerald-tinted crepe gown.

Michael had held it against her. "With your red hair, the color is perfect on you. I'm a total ignoramus where women's clothes are concerned, but I like this."

"I do, too." She had laughed. "It's a bit different. Maybe it started out to be a sari and the person who designed it ran out of fabric."

Michael had kissed the tip of her nose. "I'm going to buy this would-be sari for my sweet Sari."

Now, she closed her heart against the dull ache that persisted in following every thought of him. The Village seemed light years away as Ron's brows arched and he produced another extravagant compliment on her appearance. "Actually, Miss Wyatt, you'd look good in anything, even a gunny sack."

Sari had to admit to herself that Ron was pleasing to look at: a study in sartorial splendor with a light tan suede shirt that hung well on his broad shoulders, orange scarf at the neck, forest green slacks and dark brown ankle boots. When he threw back his head to roar with laughter, which was often, his teeth gleamed white in the glow from the candelabra on the trestle table.

Nevertheless, Sari found it impossible to be at ease. Monty, presiding in dour silence at his end of the board, wore a perpetual scowl, brooding and clearing his throat.

His wife was just as taciturn, speaking only when instructing the butler. There were two bright red spots high on her delicate cheekbones and her eyes darted ceaselessly from Ron to Sari. And from Sari to Ron. All resemblance to winsome Little Orphan Annie was erased by the ugly crease that stayed on her forehead throughout the meal. Jessica seemed closed in with her own thoughts which, Sari suspected, most assuredly included Oscar Drayton.

Was the acting mistress of the manor anxious about the older man's health or did she fear her employer's wrath, which would be dumped on her when the Duchess returned to find them all in this worrisome predicament?

The five-course meal finally wound down, and Jessica pushed back her demitasse cup. With a short "Good night" and a wave, she stalked out of the room, followed by her husband.

"Don't mind my cousin," Ron said. "Jessica takes her responsibility for the smooth running of this place very seriously. Naturally, she feels terrible about what happened to Oscar, and she's worked herself into a headache. So I guess we'll have to entertain ourselves. Are you up for a stroll in the moonlight?"

"Sure." What harm could there be in a "stroll in the moonlight" with Ron? She didn't resist when he led her from the castle to the cobblestone drive. His voice was warm when he spoke.

"I've been trying to find the nerve to say something to you. I was rotten to you this morning, and I should never treat you that way. Sari, if you say you were followed through the halls, I believe you. I'm sorry it's taken me so long to get around to admitting it. Am I forgiven?"

"I've already forgotten it." Sari was pleased by the unexpected apology. She was also forgetting her determination to keep Ron at arm's length. As they proceeded past the swimming pool, it seemed right and natural for him to draw her hand through the crook of his elbow and cover it with his own.

She was enthralled with the beauty of the Arizona night and the fragrance of the mimosa planted between the taller trees on the drive. She found herself waiting to hear him say something in keeping with the romantic aura of the setting. So she was speechless when Ron asked, "So what did Monty tell you about the castle's watch dogs?" He had halted just beyond the protruding tower and indicated a pair of tall metal gates.

"This is one entrance to the kennels," he explained and gave a low whistle that brought two shadows bounding up the ramp.

"Those can't be dogs." Sari shuddered and took a step backward. "They look like baby elephants."

"I guess you never saw a bullmastiff before. They're super-intelligent animals. Also one of the most aggressive breed of dog. They know me, so as long as you stick close to me, they might even let you pet them."

"It's nothing personal, but I really don't hanker to get to know them." Ron gave Sari a sidelong glance.

"Why is that?"

"Oh, it's just something that happened ages ago. I had gone with my mom to the bazaar. Dogs in India are allowed to run free, just like the cows. A mongrel jumped up on me and helped himself to a piece of my arm. See, there's the scar. Fortunately, the cur wasn't rabid, but ever since then, I've taken a very dim view of all canines."

Ron lifted her arm and pressed his lips to the faint mark, and the intensity of her response to this tender gesture was enough to make Sari's cheeks tingle. She quickly pulled away from him; then, annoyed with herself, she wondered why she had done so. She sighed. She didn't understand her own feelings any more.

"Sari, you're probably wary of these brutes because of their size, but I bet you'd feel differently about your grandmother's bullterriers. Pampered little critters," Ron scoffed. "They're small, but she maintains she feels safe when they're with her."

"I don't care how small they are. I think I'll keep my

distance, thank you very much."

As she and Ron leisurely retraced their steps past the leaf-covered castle walls toward the front entrance, Sari moved off the path. She tilted her head.

"Wait. I want to look up at the castle from this angle." She sighed, "Imagine waking up every morning of your life in a place like this. Do you ever find yourself thinking it's all just a mirage that's going to disappear in a pouf of smoke?"

"And where would that leave us? I like being here with you." His mustache tickled her ear as he whispered, "Sari, I want to know you—everything about you."

"Why?"

"Just because. Why don't you begin by telling me about yourself? Why haven't I met you before now?"

"Actually, that's a long story." And I don't know any of it, she thought. I don't know the beginning or the middle and especially—the end. That's why I'm here. "A long story," she repeated.

"No sweat. We have all the time in the world, but I really do want to hear it."

"Ron, I just want to enjoy looking at the castle. Why spoil it? This is a fabulous place. And dangerous! I can't get Mr. Drayton out of my mind. Who would want to do him harm? Who'd want to hurt that nice man?"

"Yeah, he's a lovable teddy bear. I am, too."

"Poor Oscar. I..." Abruptly, all thought of her grandmother's attorney was banished from Sari's mind by the flickering of a light in the top of the castle.

Chapter Nine

"Did you see it?" Sari clutched Ron's arm.

"All I see is you."

"Ron, please be serious. The light. Up there in one of the rooms on the third floor, maybe in the tower. Oh, I don't know!" She sighed. "Now it's gone."

"Didn't they tell you? The Duchess is quite an entertainer, but she hasn't used anything above the second story for ages. In your sight-seeing today, you saw some of those short flights of steps, didn't you?"

"Yes."

"The light you saw just now was probably a maid searching in a closet at the top of one of those sets of steps. But on the second floor. What you saw was, well, like a mirage. An illusion."

"If you say so." But Sari didn't believe Ron. For that matter, why should she believe Monty or Marianne who also insisted the top floor was closed off? "I just thought it might explain the whisp..." He turned sharply, and she bit off the word.

"The what?"

"Nothing, Ron." She wouldn't tell him about the whispers, at least not yet. And Ron would only laugh at her if she told him this castle was right out of one of the mystery novels she enjoyed reading. This time, though, the story was reading too true-to-life and Sari was not sure she liked this fact.

Later, as she prepared for bed, she wished she had a sleeping pill. She didn't relish the thought of another sleepless night. Above all, she didn't want to dwell on the possible connection between the wavering light she had seen and the mumbling she had heard from the stones behind the four-poster.

With the door bolted and barricaded, Sari dropped onto the soft mattress. She had barely begun to unwind when she bounced back up.

The air was quivering with sound—a sighing sound. It was not menacing in the least, but musical. It reminded her of the murmur of the sultry breeze when it teased the tall sunflowers beside Sari's home on the Indian plain. Eagerly she jumped out of bed and ran around the room in an effort to trace the strange vibrations.

From the lookout on the mountain she had noted the vertical apertures in the side of this round tower and now, as she stared in amazement at one of them, she wondered what the fighting men who had crouched behind such slits in olden days would say about this one.

It was so adroitly camouflaged that, here on the inside, it appeared to be merely a fancy, fretted section of paneling. Sari leaned closer to run her fingers over the intricate filigree stonework that had been fitted into the opening. Then she was able to identify the curious phenomenon and knew why she was being treated to a mini-serenade.

If this was another of Oliver Griffith-Rhys's fabrications, he had truly been a visionary. It was a wind chime.

Sari marveled at the music created from the opening

in the stone wall interlaced with fine wire, small odd-shaped bits of glass, even strips of tin and many tiny crystal-like stones.

A strong wind was to blame. It had begun blowing within the past hour and was fingering its way into this unique contraption to emerge, by some freak of acoustics, in hazy notes that skipped up and down and around at the will of the wind.

Why hadn't the housekeeper mentioned this original wind chime? It was a definite improvement over the secretive whispery sounds that came from the stones behind her bed. With a relieved shrug, Sari snuggled again in her featherbed and was rocked in the arms of that uncanny, ethereal lullaby until she fell asleep.

Feeling refreshed, rather than tired and irked as she had the previous morning, Sari was on the balcony early doing her exercises. After living in a congested decaying metropolitan area for eight years, she had almost forgotten there were unspoiled places free of pollution, where the view didn't consist of dried-up bushes in rusty pots and overflowing garbage cans on the sidewalk.

She drank in the beauty of the tranquil tree-shaded drive mirrored in the swimming pool and grinned when the cuckoo darted out of his little shingled house to herald the day. She stretched lazily. She had no subway to catch, no reason to move off this balcony; not unless the Duchess had returned. "In that case," Sari scolded herself, "I shouldn't be dilly-dallying."

Just then, she spied Marianne down below and waved. "Hi! Did my grandmother get home?"

"No, not yet." Disappointment was plain on the maid's face.

"I'm going to do something about that," Sari declared. "By the time I have a cup of coffee, Mr. Drayton should be awake. He's the legal mind around here. He'll know the steps we ought to take to locate her."

"Sounds like a bully idea," Marianne responded.

But things did not work out the way Sari hoped. The girl on duty, with a finger to her lips, came on tiptoe to answer her knock on Oscar's door.

"He had a pretty fair night," she reported in a low voice and waved toward the bed. "He's still sleeping."

"So he's not in any pain? I'm so glad. I wouldn't dream of disturbing him, so I'll run along," Sari told her. "Maybe he'll be awake when I drop by later. Just tell him I asked about him."

She quietly went on her way. Oscar had not looked at all well. His color was like curdled milk and his moonface was caved in. It was so unfair. What had he done to deserve this?

Sari realized with all that had happened—prowlers at midnight, spooky whispers, a daytime stalker, the attack on the lawyer, plus the prolonged absence of the Duchess—she needed to get a new perspective on everything.

No matter what Marianne said about the roof being off limits, she'd make a stab at finding some way to reach it. The place to start was with Jessica.

Sari found the housekeeper in the formal drawing room behind the gallery, where one wall was almost entirely taken up with deep cupboards decorated with Gothic traceries—fine line drawings of delicate leaves.

Red velvet drapes picked up the rich hues in the Oriental rugs and the Louis XIV couches swathed in rich damask. It was a splendid chamber and hardly the place she expected to find Jessica bent over a portable sewing machine.

"Good morning! What are you working on?"

Jessica looked up with a grimace. "It's a dull job. I'm making some new curtains, the kind with brass rings. They hang on round rods. You know, café curtains. But, this isn't your problem, is it? Were you looking for something?"

"Yes, for you. I want to ask you a question." Sari flipped a thumb. "It's about the roof."

"You mean, our ancient battlements?" Jessica leaned back in her chair and ran a hand through her short curls. "And why on earth is that?"

"I just have this yen to see what it's like up there. When I didn't get any help from Marianne, I figured you'd be the one who can show me how to do it."

"Sari, I hate to disappoint you. There is no way. Well, there are some steps that go up from inside the tower room above yours, but, by orders of Her Highness, nobody is allowed on that floor." Jessica snapped at a thread. "My idea, actually. You know how prices, including heating oil and electricity, are escalating. Needless to say, your grandma was very pleased with my suggestion to cut costs, and she lost no time getting workmen in to seal off the third story."

"Excuse me, Jessica, but last night I distinctly saw a light in one of the windows. So someone must have been there."

Jessica smiled indulgently and motioned for Sari to follow her to the front end of the gallery to an oak door that opened onto a blank wall. With her fists, the housekeeper banged on the rough surface.

"Behind these bricks is a stairway, the only access to the third floor and the tower, but this barricade is so tight a draft couldn't squeeze through. I know this is a disappointment for you, Sari, and I wish I could do something about it."

In silence they returned to the drawing room. When Jessica resumed her place in front of the machine, Sari walked over to the bay window and looked out.

What she saw was a panoramic artist's extravaganza: whipped cream August clouds under full sail above forest spires reaching for the sky. And that view should have been enough. But it was a restricted, inferior vista compared with what might be seen from the rampart.

With a sigh, Sari turned her back on the view and sank down on a cobbler's bench that flanked the window. Her attention was immediately arrested by a portrait that hung on the wall of deep cupboards to her left. As she leaned closer to inspect it, she shook her head in admiration. It was a striking study of the Duchess in muted shades of green, aqua and olive. Jessica looked up from her sewing. "Isn't that nice? She must have been around sixty when she sat for that one. It's so real, as if she's here in the flesh."

The subject of the life-sized portrait, elegantly attired in an evening gown, was commanding in appearance. The diamond and ruby tiara looked right at home on her beautifully-coifed red hair. All she lacked was a golden throne to sit upon.

"Jessica, you must have an opinion. Where do you suppose she went?"

"It's anybody's guess." The housekeeper stretched. "Well, one more seam and I'm out of here. Sorry I couldn't be of more help with the roof thing."

"I think I'll go out for a walk. At least I can look up at it."

Sari found a shady spot under a palo verde tree, sat on a lawn chair and nibbled a thumb nail. Ron Cooper had been with her on Wednesday night when she saw the light on the third floor. He insisted it was her imagination. Marianne and Monty and his wife all contended she could not have seen it because only memories lived in those shrouded rooms.

But I did see a light. No one is being honest with me, Sari told herself. I wonder why.

Her head began to throb as she listlessly gazed up at the window of the drawing room where she had seen the picture of the Duchess. That old-fashioned cobbler's bench, no more than four feet in length, had filled the space between the bay window and the painting. It was an ideal place to sit while she admired the eyes that looked real enough to blink.

As Sari squinted up at the castle, she noticed a possible discrepancy that brought a frown to her face. It looked from here as if there were no less than twelve feet of space between the window and the round tower.

If true, that meant there had to be not just one wall, but two: the wall of the tower, behind her bed, and the other, the drawing room wall of cupboards with the Duchess' portrait at the end. And in the eight feet of unaccounted space behind the painting—what was in it? Could there be a staircase leading up to the third floor tower?

Sari suddenly felt as though ice water had been siphoned into her veins. She knew that in a castle where anything is possible, it wouldn't be the first time a flight of steps and its entrance had been hidden from curious eyes.

Chapter Ten

By the time Sari rushed up the path to push through the clustering vines at the side of the castle, she had convinced herself that she would find a door. She was not disappointed. Its edges, which looked like the joining of the stones in the wall, and the rusty keyhole were both barely discernible. When she pushed against the solid plank, it was stuck. If there were stairs behind this door, they were, for the moment, out of reach.

Eager to talk to the housekeeper again, she raced to the front entrance, took the grand staircase two steps at a time, and bounded into the drawing room. Jessica, however, had finished her job and left.

Sari stepped off the distance between the bay window and wall. She felt gratified because her deductions had been on target. Her attention was captured again by the painting of the Duchess.

Impressed by the fact that this was, indeed, the work of a fine artist, she marveled that he had scrupulously given the utmost attention not only to the enormous dinner ring that graced one tapered finger, but to all the tiniest details. She examined the tucks on the dress, the silver rosettes in the chain of the necklace, and the jewels in the tiara and earrings.

He had even painted the turquoise links in her bracelet to appear so genuine that Sari could not resist rubbing their velvety surface. Suddenly one of them moved. She jerked back. She rubbed it again and watched in disbelief as the bluish-green scrap of turquoise, the color of her grandmother's luminescent eyes, began to turn beneath her touch.

Mesmerized, Sari stared as the frame that held the lifelike image shifted to one side, revealing a stairwell and a circular staircase that spiraled upwards. A shiver ran up her spine. She had found the route to the top. Nothing—and nobody—was going to stop her now.

With a foot on the sill, she heard the housekeeper's startled voice behind her. "What on earth! Is this really what I think it is? Don't tell me the painting of the Duchess is a door. How droll! It sounds just like the Duke."

"I found it by accident and it looks as though I'll get my wish, after all, doesn't it?"

"This is a joke," Jessica said, shaking her head. "There's no door at the top. I know this because before the third floor was sealed off, I was up there plenty of times. That corridor ends at the door to a tower room like the one you are staying in. And that's the only door either in or out of that room. So why these steps? It's beyond me." She chuckled.

"It reminds me of that crazy Winchester Mystery House in California. There was this eccentric woman in San Jose who built a mansion full of all sorts of oddities, like doors opening onto blank walls, fireplaces without chimneys, steps ending in midair. For a price you could go inside, but it was really spooky. Now," Jessica drawled, "let's put the Duchess back where she belongs."

"Wait. I want to go up. I'd like to see what's at the top.

And I want to go to the bottom, too. I've read about circular staircases and always wanted to experience one firsthand."

"Sari, I can't permit you to use these steps until I have Monty inspect them."

"With that railing, they look safe enough."

"True, but there may be loose or missing treads," Jessica said. "It's a long drop. Your grandma would never forgive me if you fell. Who knows how long it's been since this staircase was used? If it ever has been! And what is it for? Just for going up and down, again and again? Now that's crazy."

"But what if somebody did use these stairs and found a secret door that opens into the tower? Wouldn't that mean the third floor isn't closed off, after all? Remember, I saw a light up there."

"Have you thought it was probably the reflection of moonlight on a window?"

Sari allowed herself to be drawn back inside. As they returned the portrait into position, Jessica repeated her warning.

"That staircase is a mystery. You just better be patient until Monty gets back to you." With a wave, she left Sari nursing her frustration.

"I wonder what Jessica would have said," Sari asked herself, "if I told her I know people have been on the steps because I've heard the sound of their voices."

But she was glad she hadn't blurted out the truth or told Jessica about the secret door at the bottom of the stairway. Perhaps one of the servants and his girl friend had discovered it and decided to use the deserted third story for their romantic trysts. Why get them in trouble with Jessica?

Sari was still sitting in the drawing room when Marianne arrived, providing a welcome distraction. "I've been looking all over for you," the maid announced. Her arms were full of photo albums. "See, I've got the clipping books and I wondered if you'd care to look at them."

"Why not?" Gratefully, Sari shook herself out of her reflective mood.

"Let's go down to the library." Marianne led the way to the enormous chamber that Sari had visited yesterday morning. Sari thought the Early American decor and floor-to-ceiling shelves loaded with books would delight any bibliophile. There were roomy, chintz-covered sofas and chairs, a couple desks, lots of reading lamps, and a rock fireplace laid with logs ready for the match. She had liked this room immediately. Marianne chose a sofa beneath a floor lamp and Sari took her place beside her.

"So what are clipping books?"

"Glorified scrapbooks, actually. A history of your grandmother. Sari, I really miss her terribly. I always spend my time puttering about in her suite, bringing in fresh flowers, dusting, that sort of thing. I guess she took her little dogs with her, so now I don't even have them to care for. That's why I got out these albums—in the hope that looking at them together might take the edge off our sorrow over her absence." Marianne sniffled, "If I feel bad, I can imagine how upset you must be. So, maybe the clipping books will help us both."

"You said something about dogs. You mean the bullterriers?" Sari squirmed. She felt no sorrow, only annoyance.

"That's right." The maid turned pages until she came to some enlarged photographs. "The Duchess entered them, as usual, in the Westminster Kennel Club Dog Show a year ago. Winston and Churchill. Aren't they the cutest things ever?"

With a smile Marianne waited for Sari to ask if she were serious. Sari did not fail her. "Those really are their names? Winston and Churchill? You're pulling my leg."

"Not at all. The Duchess is an admirer of the great

man. He safeguarded England—and her pets protect her. I think it's very fitting."

Sari pictured the pint-sized pups yapping at the heels of a thief but stifled her laughter. She decided against sharing her thoughts with Marianne, who obviously adored the dogs. Why tell her she had doubts about the security such Lilliputian animals could afford? Instead, Sari tapped the books and said, "I guess these would come in handy if she wanted to write her memoirs."

"Exactly, because they're a story about her."

And, Sari soon learned, they were a story about someone else, as well: Monty.

Surprisingly, Marianne blushed when Sari pointed to a five by seven photo. "Don't tell me. Is this Monty?"

"Yes," the maid said. "He was seventeen, just after the Duchess brought him over to America."

"Wow. He was great looking, even then. And you know, he's one of those men who doesn't change much with the years, isn't he?"

"Only for the better." The maid's dimples flashed. The photographed likeness wore a bashful grin, not unlike that of a boy who has just found his own personal, filled-to-the-top cookie jar.

And why not? Sari reflected. The Duchess' kindness opened up a whole new world for him. No more scrounging in the trash for a bite to eat to keep body and soul together. Good-bye to sleeping covered with newspapers in an alley. Monty had struck it rich when the wealthy philanthropist stooped to perform a good deed on his behalf.

Marianne's blush was explained when Sari learned that he and the rosy-cheeked girl sitting at her side had been in love. "We had been seriously talking about marriage," she confessed shyly. "Everything was coming up moonlight and roses until Monty went into Prescott one weekend and met up with Jessica. I never stood a chance after that." The maid's voice had an undercurrent of longing.

"Don't get me wrong, I like Jessica, but how could he forget all the good times you two had enjoyed?" Sari said indignantly. "You'd think the common roots you share would be worth something."

"Oh, I guess it was because Jessica was so different from anyone Monty had ever known, and she bowled him over. She was, as they say here, so laid back. A real Westerner. And that's what Monty wanted to be." Marianne sighed. "If you can believe it, Jessica is the daughter of a prospector. She says he and his partner worked claims all over Arizona, over the hill from us in Jerome for one. I've heard her tell all about some of his big strikes, like what she calls 'picture rock.' That's white quartz so laced with threads of gold that you have to twist the pieces to get the metal to separate."

"He was a real miner?"

"That he was. Jessica boasts that some of his mines were so far down in the earth you wouldn't believe it. You've noticed that locket of hers? Her dad had it made for her. The wee chunk of gold in it is the real stuff. Sari, you should get her to talk about her dad. He must have been a real 'bad luck Charlie,' always a hair late in registering a claim, or cracking his skull on the tunnel walls, or getting into fights with other eager miners. Jessica grew up here in the Southwest; she was even named Rodeo Queen. How could I ever hope to compete with her for Monty?"

Sari frowned. She wondered if Marianne saw the irony of the situation. This bubbly English girl was exactly the sort of wife who would suit the chauffeur on all counts, but he had allowed himself to be roped and tied by someone who didn't share the most basic thing in his life—his pride in this castle where he'd chosen to live.

"Tell me something," Sari said. "This place is run differently from what one would expect. For example,

Monty and Jessica seem more like the owners, yet they're only employees. Do things follow this same pattern when my grandmother is on the premises?"

"Certainly, since they are not employees. They don't belong 'below stairs.' Monty is the Duchess' son, her adopted son, that is. Sari, why are you looking at me like that?"

"Adopted? She adopted him? I didn't know."

"Really?" Marianne looked bewildered. "Sari, the Duchess is always too kind by half. And it's true, she did adopt Monty. She put him through Arizona State University. The only repayment she asked was his undivided loyalty and love, which he has given a thousand times over. He shows it in the way he handles her affairs here and at the Northumberland estate where he spends a fair bit of time. Anyone would say Monty has been a very good son to the Duchess."

So stunned that she felt like a washer that stops in the middle of the spin cycle, Sari fought to straighten out the tangle of her thoughts, with one electrifying fact surfacing: Monty was her uncle.

"Well," she declared grimly, "that explains it."

"Explains what?"

"Everything. No wonder Monty looked at me so strangely at Sky Harbor when I asked him if he was one of the hired hands. I got the fleeting impression of something really peculiar about his I.D. Now I realize what it was. It was his name: Montegue Hudspith. My grandmother even gave him a family name."

This bolt out of the blue shed a bright light on why Monty could well be the one who had harassed her. Naturally, Sari reminded herself, he would be expecting to inherit his adoptive mother's wealth—lands, homes, foreign holdings, investments. All of it. And out of nowhere, on the eve of possible impending change, a granddaughter had materialized.

If I were in his boots, Sari thought, I'd be working

overtime, too, to make the interloper turn tail and run. She would take nothing—ever—from the Duchess, but of course Monty didn't know this. No wonder her presence was making her uncle jittery.

Chapter Eleven

As if she could read Sari's thoughts, Marianne said softly, "Monty is a beautiful person. Everyone has the greatest respect for him. When you get to know him, you will, too."

I sincerely doubt that, Sari thought bitterly. "Marianne, do you like mysteries?"

"Sometimes. Why do you ask?"

"Hudspith Castle seems to be full of them. You told me the top story is not occupied, but last night around eleven I saw a light up there. How's that for a mystery?"

"A light?" Marianne's astonishment could not have been contrived. For a brief moment Sari caught a glimpse of her that she never would have thought existed: that rosy-cheeked face lost its innocent expression and assumed one that would have frightened Sari had she been Marianne's enemy. It was there, it blazed, then it was gone.

"It's true. Ron and I were walking outside, and I looked up at the castle just in time to see the light before it disappeared. And something else: Marianne, tell me—did you know there's a circular staircase behind the drum tower?"

This time the English girl nearly choked. She recovered immediately but her glance was suddenly sharp, as was her voice. "No, I didn't know that. A circular staircase? My goodness, this means the only way to the upper story isn't behind the bricked-up door on the gallery. So, have you been to the roof of the castle?"

"No such luck. Jessica caught me in the very act of starting up. She said the corridor ends at the tower room and there's no door in there that would open out onto the steps. This means the staircase leads nowhere. When I said I wanted to go up anyway and see for myself, she said the staircase could be very precarious. She warned me not to try it."

"Jessica should know."

"Not really; she hadn't ever seen it. She still insists the light I saw was nothing but my imagination, but I believe the two—the circular staircase and the light—are connected." Sari laughed. "When her back is turned, I'm going up. Do you want to come with me?"

But she had lost Marianne. There were white lines around the soft mouth and the maid was staring into space. Sari finally nudged her and, flipping the pages of an album, stopped at a photo of two men seated beside a fish pond.

"Who are these fine-looking gentlemen?"

"Who? Oh, those are the Wyatt cousins. Geoffrey and Andrew. The one on the right is your grandfather Geoff. They lived in manor houses on either side of Hudspith Castle, and they were both besotted with your grandma, but passionately! They were handsome. They had dark hair and eyebrows, and they were dashing and charming as could be. In temperament, though, they were as unalike as two peas in separate pods, since Andrew was studious and introspective while Geoffrey was gregarious and jocular—like Ron Cooper, if you get my drift."

"My grandmother chose Geoffrey."

"That she did. I think it was a close race. The rivalry

between them was so exciting, people all over the county began placing bets as to which cousin would win her hand. Andrew finally announced he was fed up, packed his gear, and cleared out. Nothing was ever heard of him after he disappeared into parts unknown. The Duchess must have wanted a change, too, because she also decided to leave. She went up to some distant aunt's on the Scottish moors."

"How come you know so much about this ancient history?"

"I got it straight from the horse's mouth." The maid giggled. "My grandma was chief housekeeper at the Castle Hudspith, and she knew all that had gone on 'above stairs' as well as in the servants' quarters. She never forgot any of the fascinating details, and she was a great storyteller.

"Granny said that after the Duchess departed, the castle became a dull, dreary place. Everyone missed the parties and the arguments and competition between the two suitors. Well, you can imagine the surprise about three years later when the Duchess and Geoffrey came riding into the courtyard with the news that they were going to be married. All that part of Northumberland began celebrating. There were garden fetes with colorful tents, costume parties and bridal showers." Marianne clasped her hands in delight.

"The wedding was the talk of the year. It must have been really posh. It took place on the lawns beyond the moat—a real moat, Sari—with lily pads floating in it. The drawbridge was the flower-strewn pathway the bride and her attendants crossed to meet Geoff and his groomsmen, and at the moment of the 'amen' of the benediction, thousands of tiny roses came wafting down from the battlements."

Marianne's recital was so entertaining that Sari wished she could have been there. This was the grandmother she abhorred, yet she could not have asked the maid to stop.

"Go on, go on," Sari urged.

"So they tied the knot, and for a time all seemed to go well until the Duchess began to have a tough time with her pregnancy. She was very ill and your father, baby Sam, was born a couple months prematurely. My Gran said it was traumatic for all concerned."

She paused for such a long time that Sari prodded Marianne. "Then what?"

"Well, the little chap was sent away early, when he was barely two. He was entered at Wakefield, an elite live-in residence for children. And after that, Sam was always enrolled in boys' boarding schools." The maid frowned, "He was never kept at home much."

"Two...two years old," Sari sputtered. "I don't believe it. Couldn't she have hired a nanny, like everybody else, to look after him?"

"I'm sorry," Marianne said, nodding somberly. "I've always thought it was rather strange, but I guess it was just the Duchess' way."

"I've known several couples who wanted to be free to spend an endless honeymoon on their private little cloud nine. They were so content with each other they never seemed to need anyone else, much less a baby. Do you think my dad's parents were like that?"

"I'm not sure. Now that I think about it, Granny never seemed to say much about what went on after your father's birth."

"Oscar Drayton told me this was not one of those marriages that was 'made in heaven.' But sometimes a precious little bundle of joy can work miracles," Sari said. "I wonder what went wrong. Marianne, let me see those clipping books." Handing over the albums she had begun stacking, the maid watched curiously as Sari scanned through them.

"Weird," Sari said, and shook her head.

"What's weird?"

"No pictures. Marianne, there are no pictures of my

dad. Didn't you ever notice this? My grandmother has pictures of everyone and everything else, even her dogs, but none of my father."

"To be honest, yes, I did notice it."

"There aren't even any baby pictures. I'd love to know what he looked like as a little tyke and as a rough and tumble boy. And as a teenager. It's unnatural, that's what it is. You've seen those accordion-type snapshot collections—lots of mothers carry them. They pull them out and are so proud to show off their kids. Every mom I've known is always snapping pictures of her offspring, but my father's mother never bothered."

"It does seem so." The maid looked at Sari sympathetically. "Perhaps you can learn more about it from Monty, since he has been so close, like a real son to her."

The suggestion, kindly intentioned though it was, pricked Sari's sensitivities like a sharp pin. Now that she was aware of his true identity, discussing any personal matter with Monty was out of the question. She'd bide her time. Sooner or later she'd confront the one who had closed her heart against her own child, then supplanted him with a vagrant off the streets.

The silence that had dropped over the library was cheerfully dispelled by the tall clock playing its chimes. "We've chattered nineteen to the dozen, haven't we? I've enjoyed it a lot, but it's time for lunch," Marianne said. She ran her tongue over her lips. "Our cook does a fantastic creamy cucumber soup. It's served with a crisp green salad and salmon roulade. That's what's on for lunch. You'll love it."

Sari had had about all of her grandmother's past she could tolerate in one sitting. "Okay by me. Let's go."

At the door, Marianne paused. "Say, was the entrance you found camouflaged? I mean, are the steps to the circular staircase behind a mantel or something?" She sounded irritated and Sari didn't blame her. Marianne lived in the castle; yet a stranger, who was only passing through, had uncovered one of its tantalizing secrets.

"There is a perfectly proper secret door at the very bottom of the castle wall, concealed behind the greenery. If you didn't know what you're looking for, you'd never see it. But I stumbled on another door just before you showed up in the drawing room and found me sitting on the deacon's bench. Marianne, it's that big portrait of my grandmother. The latch is triggered by one of the turquoise links in her bracelet." Sari made a wide gesture. "You push it and presto! Open Sesame."

Looking dazed, Marianne turned off the lamp, finished gathering up the volumes and exited quickly while Sari, her mind busy with what she had seen in the clipping books, made her way to the dining room.

An hour later, as she lay in her hammock, Sari was still thinking about the books. Things just didn't add up. At first glance, everything sounded so good: take two young people in love embarking on a life together; put them into the castle the bride has inherited and pile on all the money they will possibly ever need. The couple learns they are going to have a child. The little one is born, then nearly slips away from them, but survives to make life complete for his doting parents. Camelot.

It was all so positive, but this was not how the scenario read. Sari wondered if their son had become the unwitting cause of marital friction. It would not be the first time this sort of thing had happened. In the Crisis Center she had worked with such cases where she had to sift out pertinent data. She bounced up, setting the hammock into a wild swaying motion.

"I'm doing it now!" she exclaimed. Her mind had begun the familiar task of compiling a history. Automatically, she had started to correlate the information she had picked up in the library. What set apart this off-the-cuff but nonetheless real "case" was the name on the file: My Grandmother.

Sari's thoughts went back to some of the women she had counseled. Troubled wives, battered women, discontented unfulfilled women, mothers so confused they couldn't find the courage to confront their seemingly insurmountable difficulties.

Some of them had sunk so low they had reneged on their role as mothers. "Like Daddy's mother did," Sari snorted. "Marianne surely hit the bull's-eye when she said the Duchess is standing in the need of prayer."

Sari knew she would never get over the shock of hearing that her father had been banished at the tender age of two to the institutional regime of a boarding school. Why hadn't the Duchess waited at least a few years until he reached the official age when English children were required to attend school?

Added to what Sari already knew—that at the end, his mother had disinherited him—the Duchess was emerging as the complete opposite of the charitable caring person many believed her to be.

And what about the dearth of pictures? That was the most puzzling question of all. Irritated, Sari rubbed the back of her neck. She was disgusted with herself for permitting something like this to disrupt the peace, tenuous at best, that she felt when she stepped onto her balcony.

She thought of the pine trees she'd noticed on Tuesday afternoon. They blanketed the slopes behind the castle, offering serenity and refuge from the building that could be, depending on the mood of the moment, warm and cozy or foreboding and chilly. At this moment she was badly in need of just such a sanctuary.

A brisk walk under those boughs would restore her sagging spirits. But before heading for the hills, she would see if Oscar Drayton was well enough for a visit.

Sari felt a surge of optimism when she reached the lawyer's room, peeked in, and saw no one except the patient. This seemed to be a good omen, since the girl on duty surely would not have left him if he weren't out of danger. Leaning over the bed, she called softly, "Hey, sleepyhead, can you hear me? Look at me, Oscar."

"Sari, I'm glad to see you." He peered blurrily up at her as his hand moved to clutch hers.

"How are you doing?"

"I'm not sure. I think Jessica has me on pain killers because I keep floating away. Please, can you lean a little closer. I want to tell you something." He winced as he turned his head toward her.

"Maybe this isn't a good time. After all, that was a nasty accident you had."

"No! Sari, it was not an accident."

Chapter Twelve

"Not an accident?" Alarmed, Sari stared at Oscar. Was he hallucinating? Sweat glistened on the attorney's forehead, and she reached for a tissue and dabbed at it. "Oscar, do you know who did this to you?"

He made an effort to shrug. "Don't worry about that now. What I want to talk about is your grandmother. I've been thinking about her and how odd it is that she hasn't returned. I'm sure she would have wanted to be here spiffing things up for your expected arrival on Friday—tomorrow. Sari, I need to warn you." Whatever he was about to say was cut off when Jessica, preceded by the sound of her angry voice, flew into the room.

"Why can't I trust you to do your job?" Jessica scolded the girl at her heels. "Wendy, you left your post, and I want to know why."

"I only ran down to the pantry to get Mr. Drayton some orange juice." Twisting her hands together, the maid added, "Jessica, I'm sorry, but he was dozing, and I thought he'd be all right."

"You thought! Now, go and send Polly up here. Maybe she'll be able to follow my orders."

Red-faced, Wendy scuttled out just as the tall figure

of Jessica's husband entered from the hall. She turned to him and said sheepishly, "I suppose you'll say you could hear me clear outdoors."

"You got that right," Monty admitted. "I did. Jess, what's this racket all about?"

"I found nobody was watching Oscar." She raised an eyebrow at Sari. "I apologize for this little scene. I've been very upset with this whole affair. After I tried to set a schedule that would give Oscar around-the-clock supervision, it really bothers me to have no cooperation. I didn't want him disturbed. I didn't want him trying to talk. No offense, Sari. I don't like to send you packing, but I believe it's best. I hope you understand."

"I concur," Monty added. "He shouldn't have any visitors."

Sari made as graceful a departure as was possible under the circumstances. With nothing but a hunch to go on, she was sure she'd seen a message in Monty's dark gaze that said he would gladly have sent her packing. Far away.

If only she could have spent a few more seconds with Oscar. Ron had assured her that the injured attorney in a lucid interval had insisted he didn't have a clue who had knifed him. But Sari hadn't bought that idea then and much less now. No, she thought, Oscar's covering for somebody. I'll have to try to talk to him again.

The prospect of a break under the pines sounded more inviting than ever and she could hardly wait to smell their perfume. She hastened downstairs and tore through the arcadia doors, across the garden, and beyond the cultivated area. Without slowing her pace, she continued over the undergrowth until the path tilted upward.

It was exhilarating to know she was nearing the heavily-wooded portion of Hudspith land that was not only thick with pines but with many other varieties of trees. As she climbed, she was enveloped in a cool world of green.

Underfoot, the ground was becoming rougher. Her trail was crisscrossed with small arroyos, studded with boulders, and littered with branches that had snapped off during heavy storms. To a city dweller, it was a veritable wilderness admirably suited to Sari's frame of mind.

As she tripped happily over the uneven terrain, she inhaled air heady with the resinous scent of the ponderosa pines. It should have been easy to forget the castle with its disquieting shadows. However, she couldn't stop her thoughts from reverting to the most recent enigma—the terror that burned in Oscar Drayton's eyes when he tried to caution her. If he was trying to tell her there was a menace in the castle, it was old news to her. She had known it all along.

Suddenly she became aware of a shift in the weather. When she had started out, the air was still languid with the heat of post-midday, but in a matter of minutes it had changed. Sari shivered in the stiff breeze. Since she couldn't read the signs present in the air or written on the patches of slate-gray sky visible between the branches of trees, she continued to climb, oblivious to all else but her need for action.

Sari was challenged by the unfamiliar heights, but she reveled in her solitude. She was startled when her ears picked up the crunch of boots on dry twigs. She turned. About twenty feet below her, another hiker was walking steadily up the trail and as she watched, he pushed back his cowboy hat and scratched his head.

She was filled with fury and terror. Monty! Was this to be a replay of yesterday's harrowing experience when he stalked her through the castle's corridors? Stepping off the track, Sari quickened her steps at an angle that took her out of his range of vision. Although frightened, she felt a wave of satisfaction. Then she realized her mistake.

The sinking in the pit of her stomach told Sari she was

lost. Her sense of direction, always less than reliable, failed her completely in this labyrinth of gullies, and trees that all looked alike. She didn't know how to find her way back to the trail but she was certain of one thing: this time, she was not giving Monty the pleasure of seeing her succumb to fright.

Just then a streak of lightning illuminated the area as though it were on fire. An eardrum-splitting clap of thunder shook the ground beneath her feet.

She had forgotten Monty's passing remark about the afternoon storms that were a fact of life in this section of the state, and that the rain came, not in friendly drops, but in torrents. She was drenched as she beat a hasty retreat toward what she hoped was the way back to civilization.

Unexpectedly, she saw a screen of thick foliage cascading down the opposite side of a shallow arroyo just ahead of her. Hoping it might provide shelter, she ignored the sharp brambles that caught at her clothing and tore her skin. She ran forward through the falling sheets of rain to duck behind the leaves. To her amazement she found herself on a narrow platform.

She had barely exhaled a sigh of relief when she was alerted to a new hazard: a creaking, cracking, splintering of rotted wood under her feet. Abruptly, she recalled the warnings she had ignored—warnings concerning a potential danger in this mountainous region. Abandoned mines.

What had Monty said about them? Oh yes! Now she remembered. When the veins dwindled, prospectors went off in search of more profitable sites and the entrances to the mines were, more often than not, left open. With a groan, Sari recollected his wry comment that nobody but a lunatic would ever wander over these booby-trapped hills.

Her heart seemed to stop as the platform began to break apart—slowly, as though it were taunting her for being so careless. The side toward the opening collapsed first, taking with it any hope of escape. In the split second before she tumbled off into space, Sari wondered how deep the shaft was and what she would find on the bottom. Death?

Screams tore from her throat as darkness closed around her. She was falling, sliding, somersaulting over and over on a journey that seemed to go on forever.

It ended when she landed with a scrunching splash in what felt like a lumpy swamp. She remained frozen to the spot until she caught her breath. Then she moved cautiously as she felt for broken bones. She found none, but she knew she would be a sight tomorrow with the bruises and scratches collected off the rocky sides of the shaft. That is, if she got out of here.

She had not imagined she would ever be glad to hear Monty's resonant voice. But when it came, sounding as though it originated from the opposite end of a long pipe, she could have cried for joy.

"Sari? I heard you screaming. Are you in one piece?"

She admired Monty's ability to manufacture such a worried tone of voice since it was he, theoretically speaking, who was to blame for her being in this jam.

"Yes, Monty," she called back hoarsely. "I think so."

"Way to go! Then will you be all right while I find someone to help me get you out?"

"I'll be okay."

"Good. Hang tight."

She could picture Monty racing down the slope in the rain. Going for help—or to keep silent? The thought made her heart pound. What if her uncle decided to just leave her here? She could die and no one would be the wiser.

She buried her head in her arms when a flying object whizzed past her face. She tried not to think about the bat that rustled back and forth, inches above her. In this huddled position, she began to shake.

"If Michael weren't into physical fitness," she whispered, "I might have been killed." Her ex-fiancé was not only a marathon runner; he had a black belt in karate. Sari was all in favor of participating in sports, but she had drawn the line at this. Michael had laughed when she lectured him on the inherent dangers in the martial arts. Then he retaliated by teaching her some of the basics.

"Karate's the best defense you can have against muggers," he insisted. He kept after her until she was able to toss him more or less proficiently onto the mat. "We don't want you to end up a cripple," he told her, "so I'm going to drill you in the proper way to fall. It's all in how you hit the mat."

She thought he was being facetious when he told her to think of herself as a dishrag. "That's right," he said. "You make yourself into a limp dishrag . Now, you try it."

"This is ridiculous," she had retorted. But under his tutelage, she had become an expert in relaxing. That skill had paid off this afternoon in the black horror of the mine shaft when she let go and, like a soggy, soapy dishrag, plopped onto the ground. Because of Michael's persistent instruction and what he considered the proper technique in taking a fall, Sari was still alive. But, she reminded herself, whether she stayed that way was now up to Monty. And God.

The still small voice that had been all but smothered deep within her consciousness repeated it again: And God. It's really up to Him, you know. Wouldn't this be a good time to reach out to Him? Come on, Sari, reach out.

Though keenly aware that she was ignoring the prompting of the Holy Spirit, she could not bring herself to "reach out." "Not now," she whispered. "Later. I'll do it later."

When a beam of light sliced through the murk and

she heard Ron yelling to someone to get a rope uncoiled, she scrambled to her feet.

"Be careful, Ron," she called up to him. "The walls are slippery, and they're studded with sharp rocks." In another moment he had slithered down on a rope and she was shading her eyes from the glare as he flashed his torch over her.

"If you aren't a sight!" he exclaimed. "Poor sweetheart." His arms tightened as she collapsed against him. "You're one lucky gal," he said. "Besides Monty's being nearby, Pete told me he saw you heading up here in spite of the storm warning that was out, so I saddled Coyote and came to find you. Well, fortunately you chose a deserted mine that seems to have only partly caved in, so it wasn't a straight shot to the bottom. Yes ma'am, you really lucked out."

In the dark, Ron did his best to gently dry her tears. He tied a knot in a rope and slipped the loop over her head and up under her arms.

"If you're wondering how I just happened to have this handy lariat, it's because Pete never allows a horse to leave the yard without a strong rope on the saddlehorn. You know, in case someone might be called upon to make like the Lone Ranger."

"I feel really foolish."

"It could happen to anybody." He found her hands, placed them on the rope, and landed a kiss on her ear. "I'm just glad we found you. Well, Tonto's up there, ready to haul away, so hold on."

At the top, Sari crawled out, forced herself to meet Monty's eyes and managed a word of gratitude, which he waved away with a laconic, "No problem, I was glad to be of help."

His expression was so blank that she felt the crawly way she had when he and his wife found her in Oscar Drayton's room. Monty acts as though he considers me a threat, she thought. But that's absurd. I'm no threat to anybody.

Chapter Thirteen

After Monty pulled the rope off of Sari, he cupped his hands and yelled into the shaft, "Here comes your lifeline, buddy. Signal when you're ready." When they heard a whistle, Monty began pulling, and a moment later Ron was crawling out onto the ground.

"I wouldn't want to do this every day. Daylight never looked so good." Ron grinned as he grabbed the horse's reins and vaulted into the saddle.

"All's well that ends well," Monty said, as he lifted Sari onto Ron's horse. Monty tipped his Stetson. "See you later. The rain is slacking off nicely, so you'll have a pleasant ride down. Cheerio."

Bewildered, Sari stared at Monty's broad back as he loped off down the trail. Why was the man so brusque one moment and in the next so cordial?

"You've been shaken up and might get woozy." Ron spoke over his shoulder. "We can't have you slithering off old Coyote, can we? So you'd better put your arms around me."

"I'm covered with mud. It will get all over you."

"It's sorta late to be worrying about mud. Come on, give me your hands."

She resisted momentarily but as soon as they started the descent, Sari knew he was right. The bruises were beginning to hurt, and her head was throbbing.

"Okay. Now lean against me, too," Ron ordered. He chuckled, "Yep, I know your beautiful hair looks as if you have globs of chocolate pudding stuck in it, but I won't mind, I promise."

She didn't need a second invitation. By the time they reached the castle and Ron helped her to dismount, she nearly fell over.

"Oh. I'm sorry," she gasped. "I didn't know I was so weak."

"Easy does it, precious. Take some deep breaths." His mustache brushed her cheek as he steadied her.

Stiffening, she slowly backed away, conscious of her aches and pains. Precious. That had been one of Michael's sweetheart names for her, the one she'd liked best.

"I'm going upstairs now. Thanks for bringing me home."

"Can you make it? Are you sure you're all right?"

"I'm fine. But I am mad. Ron, you've got to believe me. This is the second time Monty's done it. He followed me! I would never have fallen into the shaft if he had left me alone."

"Honey, Monty's being on that trail wouldn't have had anything to do with you." He wagged his head. "And forget about his following you. He doesn't heckle anyone and he would not—could not—harm a flea. It just isn't in the guy's nature." He peered closely at her. "Are you sure you feel strong enough to get to your room without help? If you'll wait until I take Coyote around to the stables, I'll go with you."

She turned down the offer. As she grabbed the carved oak railing, she climbed to the second floor, aware again of the castle's beauty. But yes, how sad that along with so many exquisite things to enjoy, such as this plushly-carpeted staircase with its perfectly-turned balusters of

Charles the Second's era, there had to be one nerve-jangling episode after another. Her uncle had tracked her through twisting passageways and he had tailed her up the mountain. Where was he now?

Because she was developing a bad case of looking-over-her-shoulder, Sari quickly staggered the last few feet to the round tower and burst into the room. Marianne, in the midst of dusting, jerked, stared at Sari's scratched face and arms and her mud-encrusted apparel and squeaked, "Oh, my goodness! You look as if you were pulled through a hedge backwards. I'm almost afraid to ask. Where have you been?"

Feeling like an escapee from a pig sty, Sari made light of her mishap. "Would you believe, at the bottom of an old abandoned mine?"

"A what?" Then, quickly, "How did that happen?" With wide eyes boring into Sari's, the maid seemed to be hanging on the answer.

"It was because my horrible...it was the storm. I was just trying to get out of the rain, and I thought it might be a cave. The platform at the top of the shaft gave way."

"So who rescued you?"

"Monty. And Ron Cooper."

"Oh. Well, Sari, don't feel too badly. You're not the first out-of-towner who's stepped into one of those holes." Marianne waited while Sari peeled off her filthy pants and top. Then she took them gingerly between thumb and forefinger and dumped the tattered clothes outside the door.

"I'll take the things downstairs to be cleaned and mended and see if the girls are making tea. There's nothing like some good Earl Grey to pick you up. I'll bring you a pot. But before I go, I'll turn on your spa. It would be a bully idea for you to loosen up the stiffness in your muscles by soaking in the whirlpool."

An hour later, Sari walked back and forth trying to marshal her muddled thoughts. There were strange happenings at the Castle Hudspith, not least of which was the fact that her grandmother was still missing.

Even if no one else was eager to delve into the mysterious disappearance, Sari, if only because she couldn't wait to shake the castle dust off her feet, had to try to track down her grandmother.

While she sipped the fragrant tea and nibbled genuine English scones dispatched by Marianne, she made a decision. She had to share her feelings with someone. Ron was the natural choice.

Setting aside the tray, Sari stepped out into the shadowy corridor and headed for the gallery. On the other side, she rapped lightly on the door leading into Ron's room. He appeared, looking glad to see her even as he leaned against the door jamb and sighed in exasperation.

"What are you doing up and around? Can't you be good and recoup your strength? Or maybe you consider tumbling down mine shafts all in a day's fun. Not that it won't be something great to tell your grandkids." He reached out and took her hands. "Now that you're here, what's on your mind?"

"I'm convinced we should stop wasting time. We've been procrastinating long enough. I'm truly afraid my grandmother has been kidnapped, and I think we should call in the police. Let's find her!"

"We talked about this, honey." Ron's golden eyebrows peaked. "Why are you allowing yourself to get so uptight?"

"I can't help being terribly worried that she hasn't shown up."

"Relax. She will. In her own time. And I don't think you want her to walk in on a bunch of cops, do you?"

"Maybe she'd be happy to know people care about her. Where in the world can she be? Incidentally, I'd like to ask her about something I came across this morning—a circular staircase."

"You're not serious."

"But I am. It's an honest-to-goodness circular staircase. Jessica was with me, and she was as amazed as I. But if there are stairs going up, what are they for? Ron, there's a tower room just like mine up there and I think that's where the steps go." The grin on Ron's handsome face became a scowl. To Sari's finely-honed sensibilities, he seemed to hesitate a tad too long, though he may only have been searching for the right words.

"And you want to prove that's where your 'light' came from, so you are going up to see. Right? Sari, you shouldn't be messing around. You might get hurt."

"Ron, do you recall how we stopped on what Monty called a 'lay-by' on the mountain and my first sight of this place left me speechless? Well, ever since then I've been intrigued by the prospect of climbing to the top of this castle, and now I just know that neat circular staircase is the way."

"Believe me, that's not a good idea."

"Why is that?"

His answer was to draw her into his arms and he was smiling, his face just inches away from hers. "Can't you guess? Ms. Sari Wyatt, I seem to have fallen for you, and I don't want the woman I care about taking any chances."

"No!" She twisted out of his embrace, then turned and said in a shaky voice, "Ron, you are trying to sidetrack me. I came to ask for your help, and I don't want to listen when you say things like that." The trouble was, she did want to listen. "So just don't."

"Okay, okay! I'll back off. For now. I only want you to know how I feel. I'm glad that you'd come to me when you're upset about the Duchess."

"I really want to find her." Sari was shocked when she realized the words she had uttered had sprung from unexpected, faint stirrings of sympathy for her grandmother.

"Monty isn't worried, as you know," Ron said, "because she often drops from sight. However, for your sake I'll convince him we should take steps to locate her." Before she could stop him, he reached over and planted a kiss on her forehead.

"You smell so good, you're irresistible."

"And you are impossible. I'm leaving."

She was closing the door when he said, "But you do feel better about the Duchess? Will you relax just a little?" She nodded.

"I can't promise anything, but I'll try."

That was Sari's intention—until she heard the whispers in the stones again.

Dinner that evening had been another dreary affair, an affront to the feast provided by the castle kitchens. Flavored with tension, the roast duck and potato-orange dumplings lost their appeal and became merely something to be dispensed with as soon as possible. But what was to follow promised to compensate for the unpleasant hour. The storm had passed over, leaving the air balmy enough for an after-dinner demitasse beside the crescent-shaped swimming pool.

"I've been wishing for a closer look at this," Sari said as Ron led her through the security fence and onto the deck with its strings of lighted Japanese lanterns and round glass-topped tables under striped umbrellas.

"Nice, huh?" The scene included underwater lighting with splashes of red, yellow, purple, and green.

"I'll say," Sari agreed. "This could be one of those swank resorts in the Poconos like the pictures you see in the Sunday papers."

"I've been here many times when friends come to visit your grandmother, and this is exactly how it always looks." Tonight, however, there was no loud laughter, no splashing or fighting over a beach ball. Sari was the solitary woman and the object of admiring glances from the one and only man present. He didn't seem to notice the spectacular blue and purple bruise on her chin.

She sipped her coffee and watched Ron tossing jelly beans into his mouth. She dodged and giggled when he aimed them her way. By the time they kicked off their shoes and were sitting on the edge of the pool with their feet dangling in the water, she felt far away from the menace within the brooding castle.

Ron reached over and brushed her bangs with his finger, trailing his hand over her cheek. He sighed huskily. "Sari, Sari. You are some special kind of lady. And to think I've not met you before now. I have a feeling that my life would've been quite different if the Duchess had told me she had a granddaughter like you hidden in the woodwork."

Abruptly, the spell was broken. Sari grabbed her sandals and fled up the steps. Behind her, she could hear Ron begging, "Wait! What did I say? Please come back." But she didn't stop until she was inside her room. She had been mellowing toward her grandmother. She was aware of this now. But Ron's sweet nothings had reminded her that the Duchess had indeed kept her hidden.

Sari's compassion was blown away; the resentment that had been shriveling took over. How could she have forgotten, even for a moment, the debt she owed her father and herself?

As she perched on the chaise, Sari reviewed her sole purpose of being in Arizona. Her mission was to remind her grandmother of what she had done and what she had left undone. And Sari was not going to allow that mission to be sidetracked or diminished.

Chapter Fourteen

There was nothing but trouble here, trouble and mystery. Only a naïve person starved for adventure would consider this castle in its sylvan setting an enviable place. "And," Sari grumbled under her breath, "I sure did fit into that category."

In reality, this was a stone super-mansion that was not at all what it pretended to be, and she could hardly wait to get away from it. Out east, her office was waiting and the sooner she winged her way back to Manhattan and her ordinary, humdrum life, the better she would like it.

She leaned back against the pillows on the chaise, mentally bidding farewell to Hudspith Castle and to this quaint room, no doubt the loveliest bedroom she would see in her lifetime. She would hate to leave it with its spongy pastel rag rug, that oval pier glass where she could see all of herself at one time, and the canopied bed that made her feel so pampered.

As she scanned the collection of children's classics that she had once adored and would love to read again, she was aware that in another minute she would lose her resolve. She blew her nose, ordered herself to straighten up, and fervently wished the wind would bring its tinkling nocturnal serenade.

But tonight there was no wind. There was no music that would release her mind from the thrall of doom. Then she heard the throbbing whispering, the haunting vibrations she had listened to once before. A chill shot up her spine. She jumped up and wrestled the four-poster away from the wall far enough to let her press her ear against the stones. On the other side, on what she now knew was the circular staircase, people were conversing. Sari's heart began to pound. No matter what the housekeeper said, if the steps were safe enough for them, they would be safe for her.

With her ear glued to the wall, she waited until the hollow tones faded downward, then tiptoed toward the drawing room. There was no one in sight as she touched the silver bracelet's turquoise link, then slipped through the doorway and hopped over the sill onto the circular staircase.

Guided by the light from the drawing room, Sari began inching her way up treads that were, contrary to what Jessica feared, sound as the proverbial dollar. When the steps ended on a landing, her heart raced.

The wall in front of her didn't look like a door but a light touch caused a section of it to open inward. She moved with it, stepping into total darkness. For a moment Sari felt panic. She wondered where she was. Then her hands touched garment bags and she laughed. It was a closet.

"How clever!" she marveled. The way in and out of this tower room was camouflaged by a closet. No wonder Jessica hadn't ever known about the spiral staircase.

In a moment Sari's hands came across a tiny recessed latch on the other side. She emerged on a scene at the same time so natural, yet totally unexpected. Her eyes widened at the sight of four girls seated around a table in the center of the chamber.

The attractive olive-skinned quartet had been playing cards, which they laid down as one of them shyly said, "Ola! Please, come in." Sari remained standing in the doorway, unable to stop staring.

"Who are you? Do you all speak English?"

"Only me." The girl who had greeted Sari smiled modestly at her. "I don't do too good, though. I am Marita. And this is Rosa, Teresa, and Berta. See, the pharmacist in our town, he is married to a lady from Texas. Since I was eleven, I work for her in their house. She ask me to teach her the Español, so I learn some English." With a graceful gesture, she waved Sari to a vacant chair. "You will sit, no?"

Sari tried to appear calm as she looked around the room. It was simply-furnished with several cots covered with bright coverlets. A shag carpet covered part of the wooden floor. Under the window (surely the one where she had seen a light), there was a kitchenette housing a midget refrigerator and hot plate. There were two doors that she supposed would open into a bathroom and the third floor corridor. In the corner she saw a flight of steps that led, hopefully, to the parapet and a view of the moon-splashed castle grounds.

"I hope you won't mind my asking, but what are you doing here?" Sari said.

Marita raised her eyebrows. "You don't know?"

"That's right. I don't know. And I'm sort of curious."

The girl pushed her black bangs out of her eyes, shrugged at a remark from one of the others. "First, how about you tell us, what is this place?"

Sari stared at the group. "Believe it or not, it's a castle."

"A castillo! You kid us, no?"

"My grandmother owns it, and I'm here on a short visit."

"Were you here when we come the other night?" Marita's dark eyes narrowed. "Why don't we see you before now?"

"I honestly have no idea what you're talking about. And you didn't answer my question." Sari smiled reassuringly. "What are you girls doing here in this castle?"

"Work. They promise us work. That's why we come to the Estados Unidos."

"Oh, I get it. You've emigrated. From Mexico?"

"Sí. These people who bring us, they arrange everything. They say they find us jobs that pay so good, we can send lots of pesos back home. Excuse me, please."

After a brief huddle, Marita flashed another smile. "We think you are different. We think we trust you."

"Thanks. Of course you can trust me."

With an eye on the door, Marita lowered her voice. "Bueno. You see, is not just jobs we want. Is Rosa's sister. Since Lupe, she come across over border, she has not send message to Rosa. The policemens in our town, well, they just wink. They say, so what? Lupe cross border with no papers in her pocket, so she take what come to her. They say she is in jail, but Rosa thinks no." Tears gathered in Marita's eyes as she leaned across the table. "This is why Rosa look for her."

"Of course she wants to look for her sister. But, you four, do you have your immigration papers? There is no problem with that?"

"Well, no, we don't have nothing like those green cards yet. But we will soon. These people who bring us here, they say we not need to go through paperwork. They say we not worry. They take care of all little red tapes."

"Oh, oh! You're here illegally." Sari frowned as she stared at the young girls.

Marita sighed. "I guess, sí. But this happen many time. Everybody, they know where people wait so we come across to meet them. They pick us up. That's how Lupe, she get here." She spread her hands in the classic Latin gesture, "It happen all the time."

"You keep saying 'these' people. Do you know their

names? Who are they?"

"Well, there is this group, six, seven, maybe more, but they don't tell us their name. They are not like some who grab people off street—runaways, kids like that. Their work, it is very good. Maybe you know, or maybe no. We have not much to hope for in our town. Sure, I could marry a peón and have his kids and help him plant corn. Señorita, who don't want chance to be model or star in videos and live in Las Vegas or maybe Hollywood."

Rosa had begun to cry and Marita added, "When Lupe, she drop out of sight, Rosa decide to meet the Gringos so she can find what happen to Lupe. We are Rosa's friends, and we no want her to come alone."

"You are all very brave," Sari said. "So, do you have any leads?"

"Leads? Oh, I see. Only some things said here and there. How do you call them, rumors? Rosa's sister, she is not first girl to disappear." Marita shivered. "But now we are here, we are getting scared. How we know what happen to us?"

Sari's heart sank as she contemplated their fresh young faces and tried to adjust to the existence of a clearing house right here in Hudspith Castle. At least that is what it looked like to her: a clearing house for unsuspecting illegal aliens en route to…where? What would be their final destination?

"Listen, I'm going to see what I can come up with," she told them. "Don't worry. I'll get back to you."

Sari tore her eyes away from the steps in the corner. All thought of climbing to the roof of the castle left her mind. It was time to do now what she should have done hours ago—raise the alarm. It would be more than a phone call to that kind fellow passenger in Prescott. This S O S would go right to the top. The Sheriff's Department.

By morning the castle would be crawling with law

men. Those responsible for the presence of Mexican citizens in the tower would be ferreted out, the motive behind the assault on Oscar Drayton would come to light, and Sari would learn why Monty was trying to frighten her away before her grandmother returned.

Carrying with her the memory of Rosa's tears, Sari hurried down the circular stairs. Her mind was already imagining how her grandmother might react when told about the Mexican girls.

Oscar had said defending the disadvantaged was one of the Duchess' greatest talents. If true, it would be just like her to dispatch a fleet of detectives to locate Rosa's sister Lupe, and then to personally deal with the Immigration and Naturalization Service on the girls' behalf. Yes, a concentrated search for the Duchess definitely needed to get underway.

Out of breath, Sari reached the great hall and the old-style, early 1900's telephone. Interrupted by the soft swish of arcadia doors sliding open, she scuttled behind one of the hulking, conveniently-situated sets of armor.

She watched as Marianne and Monty came in from the terrace and, stopping within five feet of her, whispered together. "That tower is our first concern," Monty said as he leaned against the mantel and tugged at his mustache. "We've got to decide on a course of action. Do you have any ideas? Where do we go from here?"

"I wish I knew." Peering around the edge of her cover, Sari saw that the maid, who was kneading her temples with her fists, looked as distraught as she sounded. "She's been asking all sorts of questions. I'm petrified that she—Monty, I'm afraid Sari really suspects something."

"Little Miss Curiosity." Monty gave a dry chuckle. "Yes, it is rather laughable but believe me, I'm not really amused. Sari is going to be in deep trouble unless—what's the matter?"

"Did you hear that noise?"

"Jumpy, are you? Well, old girl, that makes two of us. There is a lot on our plate, but buck up. We're in this together, and we can handle it."

Recognizing that she was the subject of their conversation, Sari had nearly given herself away by an involuntary gasp. To her relief, the couple exited into the east wing, and she was free to grab the telephone and make her call. In a few seconds she replaced the receiver on its hook. Apparently today's deluge had wrecked the wires again. The line was dead.

There was nothing left to do but retreat. She sank down on the landing, beyond caring whether anyone should find her sitting with her forehead against a newel post.

It had been shocking to see the evidence of matters dreadfully amiss in the tower, but she hadn't been prepared to hear Monty and Marianne, the soft-spoken, self-professed believer, indict themselves. That they were trafficking in Mexican citizens was enough to make Sari's stomach churn.

She had watched as Monty rested against the ancient coat of arms engraved with the words of the Hudspith family creed, words that should have meant everything to him. "That man has no loyalty," Sari said to herself. "And when the Duchess learns about this, it will break her heart. How could he do this to her?" She raised her head when the subject of her thoughts suddenly appeared at the bottom of the steps.

"Hi," she said, forcing a carefree tone. "And what are you doing up so late?"

"I could pose the same question," Monty responded. "However, I know the answer. Like some of our visitors, you have insomnia. I am never too surprised when I come across one of them, like you, knocking about at odd hours of the night. Sari, dear, I apologize, but that's how the castle affects people. Tell you what. You run along, and I'll get my wife to fetch you some hot Ovaltine.

That will help you sleep."

He helped her up. "Goodnight." How kind he sounded, remarkably solicitous of the well-being of the inquisitive young woman from Manhattan.

As Sari waited inside her room, she wondered what Jessica would do when she became aware of the situation in the tower. What would she say if she knew that Sari was afraid of her husband? In spite of herself, her eyes filled, but when she heard footsteps outside, Sari blinked away the tears.

She opened her door. A tall figure stepped in, and Sari screamed.

Chapter Fifteen

Instead of Jessica, it was Ron who, with a glance at her face, gathered her close.

"Who were you expecting? Dracula? It's only me. You poor little thing, you're completely frazzled, aren't you?" At the touch of his hands on her back, Sari's tears began to flow.

Watch out, Sari's inner voice reminded her. You are letting him comfort you again. Despite the warning, she was too keyed-up and Ron's gentle tone of voice was all she heard.

She was caged in by problems, but this fierce attraction to Ron was the most upsetting. Even while she held back, she found herself longing to be free to melt in his embrace with no thought of anyone but him.

As Ron's head came down, and she clasped her hands about his neck and lifted her face for his kiss, she remembered Michael. And the door to the dark corner of her heart where she had banished all the Michael-memories opened a tiny bit more.

"Sorry, Ron. I'm not thinking straight tonight." She dropped her arms.

"Baby, it's okay. Who's asking you to do anything as drastic as thinking? You ought to be like me and just go with the flow. I couldn't sleep. Then I remembered the moon and took a chance that you might still be up. I hoped you'd invite me to sit with you for awhile on your balcony."

"I don't think so. Do you know how late it is?"

"We've got to get rid of these worry lines." He brushed her forehead with cool fingers. "Come on, it's too beautiful a night to waste, so let's go sit on the hammock."

"Ron, I have a better idea. I think I'll share something with you. It's something I just learned, and you are going to be as shocked as I was. So will you please humor me? Sit in the armchair there."

"Sure. I don't know what could be more important than enjoying the moonlight, but go ahead. Shoot."

Lounging casually, his hands linked behind his head, Ron's eyes never left hers. But by the time Sari finished her report, his golden tan had receded, leaving his face a pasty beige.

"I just knew it would make you sick," Sari said. "This whole thing reeks of the slave trade, doesn't it? And I feel so bad about those young women upstairs." When he groaned and covered his face with his hands, she fell onto her knees in front of him. "This has really thrown you, hasn't it?"

He straightened up, and cleared his throat several times. He muttered, "It's true, just as you've got it figured."

"What? The tower really is a clearing house? How long have you known about it?"

"It probably won't make any difference now, but I'd like you to believe me when I say I didn't want you to know I had anything to do with the business. Sari, I never suspected a thing the first time I was asked to pick up some 'passengers' in Nogales."

"Wait a minute. Are you asking me to believe you

used your 18-wheeler for transporting aliens? Ron, you aren't telling me you are involved!"

"Yes, I've hauled some of them up here. Two times; no, it was three. Remember, I told you about the compartment behind the cab? That's where they'd ride. But hey, I didn't bring in the four girls who are here now. Like I told you, my rig is in the garage in Phoenix."

"How did you get away with it? Even at night, how could big vehicles like yours come and go without being noticed?"

"It was simple. We'd take the deserted back roads to where we'd park and from there we hiked."

"With those bullmastiffs on patrol duty?"

"The other guys shot tranquilizers into them, but, like you saw, the dogs and I are friends. Getting in and out of the castle was no problem, either, because there's that door at the bottom of the circular stairs. You saw how it looks just like part of the wall. Oh, man! Sari, there's big bucks in this racket, and I was in a financial bind." His voice petered out in a ragged moan. Sari was horrified by this unexpected disclosure.

"But Ron, you're smart enough to have guessed the fate that would befall some of those young girls. And my grandmother—she's a crusader. She does battle for the oppressed. When the public hears about this, her reputation will be ruined. Didn't you think what this would do to her?"

"I told you, I never meant to get sucked into it. I'd already made up my mind to quit." To her amazement, his eyes were swimming in tears. She was touched by the remorse she saw mirrored on his face.

"Now I understand why you didn't want the police or a doctor coming around. They might have gone up to the tower. Furthermore, when I heard voices on the stairs—yes, I did hear them—one of them was yours, wasn't it?" Sari swallowed hard. "No wonder you got all hot and bothered when I said I wanted to poke into corners!"

The sophisticated veneer, the "machismo" that was the Ron Cooper trademark, seemed to be stripped away, leaving him with a vulnerability that Sari found oddly appealing. She told herself Ron was not the first decent person who had succumbed to temptation. Some pity battled with the revulsion she felt.

"If I'm having trouble adjusting to the fact of what has been going on," she said, "just think how the Duchess will react when you tell her about your part in it. Because you will have to lay it all on the table. You know that, don't you?"

"I know. I love that old lady, and I really blew it this time." Ron got up and slowly walked onto the balcony, turning to give her a wistful look. "I've blown it with you, too, I guess. If you don't want to look at the moonlight with me now, I won't blame you."

She was mocking herself as she moved toward him. "Who do I think I'm fooling?" Sari asked herself. In spite of what Ron had done, she still wanted to look at the moon and count the stars with him. And she wanted him to hold her.

Ron lifted her off her feet and twirled her around. For a moment, they forgot their troubles and laughed when Sari became dizzy. However, it was more than dizziness that sobered her as she reached for the hammock and lowered herself onto it.

The most extraordinary thing was happening: for the first time in years. She was able to see the face of her mother. Clearly. How often had Sari failed as she tried to bring the blurred image into focus. Now, suddenly, it was as though that beloved form was here beside her.

The sight of the hurt, questioning expression on the sweet face of her saintly mother, at whose knee she had learned God's commandments for holy living, brought Sari back to reality. She knew what her mother would think of debonair Ron, the charming extrovert who could make her pulse trip faster.

Sari could almost hear her ask, "Sweetie, what does Ron think of our Lord?"

There was just one truthful answer and in her heart, Sari whispered it: "Mama, Ron's thoughts are very far from Him."

She longed to bury her head on her mother's shoulder, feel her squeezing tight, hear her soft voice praying. She wanted to confess that something had happened to the missionary child who had loved to sing the grand old hymns, repeat her repertoire of Bible verses, whose favorite game had been "playing church." Where had that Sari gone?

This Sari, cowering on the hammock, trembled at the touch of Ron's hand and her silly heart fluttered out of control at his glance. This Sari teetered on the brink of an emotional involvement with a man who she judged as spiritually destitute as any of the Indian nationals her parents had loved and served.

Impatiently, Ron moved forward, his hair frosted gold in the pale light, his hands outstretched. "Come to me, Sari."

Just before he touched her, she gave an involuntary shove with both feet—just enough to stop him but with the momentum of the hammock behind it.

"Aw, Sari, be nice." The wide smile disintegrated as he backed up, lost his balance, and floundered against the railing. Fumbling for support, his groping hands slid along the balustrade before he flew out into space—Ron and a section of posts and railing together in an ungainly, macabre, sprawling dance. She covered her ears against his terrified cries.

In a daze, she tumbled out of the hammock. She tried to scream but no sound came out and before she could gather her wits, Monty was there. He entered at a gallop, deposited a sloshing cup of Ovaltine on the desk, then dropped to his knees to peer through the gap in the balustrade. Speaking over his shoulder, he barred her way. "If you're thinking of coming any closer, don't. Not unless you want to join him down there."

"Oh, poor Ron. He's not dead, is he? Please don't tell me he's dead." Tears flowed down her flushed cheeks.

"No, I don't think he is, thanks to the bushes that broke his fall. Now, just what went on here?"

"You can stop looking at me like that. It was an accident, pure and simple." Sari mopped at her cheeks. "I pushed him and the railing broke loose and he went over. I didn't do anything on purpose."

"Don't worry, I believe you." Monty's brows came together as he scowled. Sari was smitten by the cold fury in his dark eyes as he turned and called down to the men who had come running from behind the castle. "He's okay? Good job. Fellows, get him into bed, and I'll be along shortly."

Ushering her inside, Sari's uncle said grimly, "I do not want you stirring out of here, and do not open—repeat, do not open—the hall door for anyone. Do you think you can promise me this?"

"I have no intention of venturing from these safe confines," she replied tartly. "But I don't know why you should care."

"Don't you, now? Hasn't it occurred to you that the balustrade might jolly well have been tampered with? Oh, not enough to break, but made just loose enough to give you a good scare? Tough luck for Ron. He's heavier than you, and it gave out under him."

"I don't know what you mean. This morning it was perfectly solid."

"Yes, and everybody knows how taken you've been with that balcony. It's no secret that the first thing you do in the morning and your final act at night is to go out there, lean against the railing and drink in the 'invigorating' air."

She suddenly recalled the last time she had sung her balcony's praises; no one had laughed. Was it because somebody had already decided to sabotage it?

"I agree that someone may be trying to scare me off. Whoever it is, he just can't wait until I leave here. But aren't you a bit leery that you might be on the list of suspects? What if I tell that I know you have been shadowing me ever since I arrived?" Sari actually enjoyed watching Monty squirm. Or was it anger that caused his mouth to twitch.

"Come off it," he growled. "Young lady, it would be a big help if you could begin to trust me."

"You don't honestly expect me to trust you!" After what Sari had overheard in the hall, his remark was an insult.

"Yeah. Right. I guess that is too much to ask," he admitted sourly. "For what it's worth, let me tell you the Duchess is the only real mother I've ever known, and I love her. When she said she had asked you to come, I was glad. Regardless of how it must appear to you, I wish you only the best."

His impassioned speech stirred Sari, but she was plagued by too many doubts and unanswered questions. How could she trust this man who invariably was lurking nearby every time danger threatened?

"I'll wait for you to lock your door. And don't—" Monty never finished the sentence. It was severed by a high-pitched scream that echoed through the corridors. "Oh brother," he sputtered. "Not again! That came from Oscar's room."

Chapter Sixteen

Shivery tingles skipped up Sari's spine and without a second thought she was out of the tower, running behind Monty toward the gallery, around it, and down passageways leading to the lawyer's bedroom.

Panting, she watched as Monty lunged through the open doorway, sidestepping the unexpected tableau: Oscar prone on the floor and the maid, Polly, with a wet towel in her hands, bending over him.

"Monty, I'm so ashamed of going to pieces. When I came in to give him his medicine, I found Mr. Drayton out cold, and I just panicked. I'm so sorry."

"You're a good nurse, Polly. It's not your fault that I fainted," Oscar told her and flapped a hand. "Help me up, Monty, will you?"

Once more between the sheets and propped against a pillow, color started to come back into Oscar's cheeks and he was able to joke. "They say there's a first time for everything, but who'd think I'd do something so silly? However, now that Sari's here, I'd like to talk to her—alone."

He waited until the others left, not without one of

Monty's enigmatic glances in Sari's direction. Then Oscar patted the side of the bed.

"Come and sit here. The truth about this humiliating event is that I was just on my way to see you when I keeled over."

"You were doing what?"

"I thought I could make it; guess I was wrong." He grimaced. "Sari, I wanted to run something by you. Ever since I learned the Duchess was missing, I really haven't been fretting. One can't be one hundred percent sure that some psycho wouldn't be prowling about, even in this rather secluded wilderness, but my gut instinct tells me she hasn't encountered any such misfortune. However, her staying away so long doesn't sound like her. I've been thinking, and I've come up with an idea. Sari, I sincerely hope that I'm correct in thinking she's right here—in her own personal hideout."

"A hideout? In the castle?"

"Why not? What respectable castle doesn't have a secret room to which one can slip if the need presents itself? You, of all people, should know that. Well, on Tuesday morning a bit of peace and quiet might have sounded good to the Duchess. So, using the gazebo as a cover and scooting low behind the hedges, she stole back inside to her private sanctum. At least, right or wrong, that's the conclusion I've reached."

"Yes, but wouldn't she have shown up before now?"

"The very issue in a nutshell. And it's beginning to bother me no end. As I said before, I'm sure the Duchess would insist on having her hand in all the preparations for your arrival. That is, unless some calamity has befallen her, such as—heaven forbid—a heart attack. Or a stroke. So, my dear, I think you must try to locate this hiding place."

The lawyer smiled at her expression of dismay. "Sari, it's either you or me, so I guess you're elected. Besides, you're the castle buff. If anyone can find her, you can.

But be on your guard. Don't trust anyone, and that includes—"

Monty chose that crucial moment to rejoin them. "Ready, Sari? I'll walk you back." There was no conversation between them until they were in front of her door and Monty killed the silence with a deep drawn-out sigh.

"Lucky Oscar. I didn't know what we'd find, but I'm glad it was only a fainting spell."

"So am I. Now, about 'lucky' Oscar and that bunkhouse affair: just suppose my grandmother's Last Will and Testament was behind it. He's her attorney. Perhaps he is here to alter it and someone decided to make it difficult, if not impossible, for him to do so."

Sari's words had the desired effect and she had Monty's full attention as she added, "That's what I figured yesterday. Now, I am tempted to believe something else was the motivating factor behind Oscar's so-called accident. Perhaps you would care to explain? I refer to what is going on upstairs." She gestured. "Up there."

"Do you mean to say you've been upstairs?" His eyes bored into her, his face bronzed granite. "Yes, so help me, that is what you are saying. And when did you make this foray into the upper regions?"

"Oh, awhile ago. Shall we compare notes on what I found in the tower?"

His reply was to wheel and stride quickly around the corner of the hallway. She wouldn't have expected him to do anything else, certainly not to admit anything. Especially to her.

Inside her room, the sight of the Ovaltine spilled on the desk brought it all back: Ron's backward plunge, the tearing sound of his screams, then Ron crumpled and inert on the cobblestones. With a moan, she threw herself onto the bed and pulled the pillow over her face.

Why wasn't she the one to fall? That's what Monty

had insinuated. It should have happened to her.

It was God. God delivered you. The words were loud and succinct, and they hovered on the threshold of Sari's mind, waiting for her to acknowledge his divine intervention.

"Yes, yes! You're right!" She threw off the pillow and raised her voice: "I know you are listening, so I'll say it. You protected me in the mine shaft and on the balcony you kept me in your hand. I don't know why you bothered, but I really am glad to still be alive. And," she added huskily, "I'm even more thankful that Ron is, too."

For a moment, the paneled walls and the organdy flounces over the four-poster faded as she remembered how it had been when she was working at the Crisis Center, where, surprisingly, no restrictions had ever been placed upon her.

She had been free to share her faith in God with those who came struggling in the throes of their own crises to find help. "But I was tongue-tied," she sadly admitted. "Just as I've been with Ron."

Groaning, she slid to the floor and staggered into the bathroom to lean over the basin and splash cold water on her face. Tipping some aspirin into her palm, she gulped it down, eyed with longing the chaise lounge, and shook her head. Not now.

This was not the time to sit quietly on that comfortable couch while she owned up to her backsliding. Or to ask God to help her feel again the joy of renewed fellowship with Him—not with this engulfing conviction that time was running out.

More than ever, Sari longed to see the Duchess walk back into the castle to take hold of the reins that seemed to have slipped from her fingers. To set things straight.

She had no doubt that if this champion of law and order were aware of what was going on in the tower, she would wade right in and begin sweeping. That is what she would do if she were still alive, if she could move. And if, Sari ruefully reflected, I can find her.

Her immersion in castle lore had placed Sari in good stead for this moment. Any secret room would need to be easily accessible from her grandmother's quarters, perhaps by means of something akin to the circular staircase so she could come and go at will. Therefore, that's where the search must begin.

Once more Sari ventured into the shrouded hallways, only to stand hesitating in front of the Duchess' door while doubts nibbled at the edges of her resolution. What gave her the right to invade the private domain of the chatelaine of the castle?

"What alternative do I have?" Sari asked herself. "If Oscar is correct and there really is a hideaway, she may be lying there, helpless and in pain."

Squaring her shoulders, she tried the handle, found the door unlocked, and walked in.

The Duchess' sitting room was just as gorgeous as Sari had anticipated. It was an eclectic jumble of period furniture: a rare Tudor movable screen with rich carving, Hepplewhite chairs, William and Mary tables with contrasting woods cleverly inlaid against a background of veneer, and so on and on.

Reluctantly, she dragged her enchanted gaze from all this beauty and got to work, pressing, probing, pulling, tapping. But the hoped-for entrance-exit did not come to light. She uncovered no sliding panels that, when nudged, would swing aside to reveal a gaping tunnel, no loose floor boards, no trap door. It was just what it appeared to be: a tastefully cluttered, lived-in sitting room.

Sari concluded that perhaps it was for some imagined, life-threatening contingency that her grandparent had been so close mouthed about a retreat, if she really had one. Affluent and powerful, possibly the frequent object of intrigue and envy, she had, without doubt, felt the need to act prudently.

Her secrecy, however, was something to be regretted, as Sari transferred the search to the adjacent bedroom and a meticulous inspection of each tiny crevice.

She hated to admit defeat but if the route peeled off this suite, it was so well disguised it would take a Houdini to find it.

Instead, she uncovered a safe.

It had been concealed behind an ornate frame edged in gold leaf rosettes that held a marriage certificate—that of the Duchess and Ollie. The door of the safe, curiously enough, was ajar. Telling herself this was just what she should have been looking for all along, she eagerly reached into the compartment and brought out a hefty pile of official-looking papers.

She spread them out on the bed, hoping to find a blueprint of the castle that would show a secret passageway, but there was none. There was something else of interest, though: four embossed documents held together by a velvet ribbon.

The one on top was a marriage certificate which she carefully unfolded. She had assumed this would be the contract between the Duchess and her first husband, Geoffrey Wyatt, but she immediately sensed something amiss. Her eyes widened. The scribbled signature beside the Duchess' dainty spidery one was not his. This name was one Sari had heard for the first time when Marianne had shown her the clipping books: Andrew Wyatt.

Even more confusing was the date on it: three years before that on the next document Sari looked at, which was the expected marriage certificate signed by Geoffrey and her grandmother.

As she turned the documents over and over in her hands, Sari tried to sort it out. No one had ever mentioned that the Duchess had been married first to Geoffrey's cousin.

And why did the fact of Andrew's demise at the age

of twenty-five as noted in the third official paper, his death certificate, seem also to have been of no consequence? Or was it because this union of a brief three years' duration had been one of the best-kept secrets of the century.

By the time Sari inspected certificate number four, she should have been beyond shock. This one was the record of her father's birth, duly attested to and sealed, with his mother's name in the allotted space. But on the line opposite, the one reserved for the baby's father, there was that name again: Andrew Wyatt.

It was too confusing. During the library session with the clipping books, Sari's brain had buzzed with questions. Now she was faced with an even more perplexing one. It was shamefully evident that her grandmother had allowed her son to go through life thinking Geoffrey was his father. She had let him grow up believing a lie. Why?

Sari's lip curled with disgust as she asked herself why she should be amazed at anything the Duchess had done or anything she'd left undone. She was one of a kind, a woman praised for her active concern for children, yet who lacked any genuine maternal feelings.

Weak with contempt, Sari came close to abandoning her efforts to find her. Clutching her father's birth certificate, she whispered, "I just can't leave here until I tell her what I think of her. She failed abysmally as a mother and, as a grandmother, she was less than human. Daddy, she's an all-around loser, and I want her to hear it from me."

Rubbing the angry tears off her face, she replaced the safe's contents and was closing the door when her heart began to hammer against her ribs. She was not alone. Someone whose footsteps were muffled by the thick rug had followed and was standing behind her.

Chapter Seventeen

"What are you doing?" The voice was low and soft.

Jerking around, Sari glared at Marianne. "You shouldn't sneak up on people."

"Forgive me. I didn't mean to startle you. You were so engrossed. Are you looking for anything in particular?"

"I'd like to be alone, if you don't mind," Sari snapped. She did not feel obliged to justify her presence in her grandmother's apartment to anyone, especially Marianne.

The maid winced, but Sari no longer cared about her feelings. This was the girl who had joined in his mirth when Monty called Sari "Little Miss Curiosity."

Marianne did not leave. She stood there with a sorrowful frown on her normally sunny face. "Just go," Sari repeated.

"Why are you treating me so coldly? Sari, you've changed."

"Yes, I have! It's not because I wanted to change. I never had a sister, and I was beginning to feel I'd found one in you. And you've spoiled it." The next words issuing from Sari's mouth were wholly unplanned, but she was powerless to stem the tide. "Girl, you really sounded sincere with all that pious talk. You asked me to join you in a pray-along for my grandmother when all the time you were in on what is happening in the tower!"

"Please stop. You've got it all wrong. Let me explain."

"It hurts to know you've been found out, doesn't it? Marianne, you can't say a thing to mitigate the shock I felt when I learned you're not as perfect as you wanted me to think."

"Oh, my goodness. Believe me, I can explain everything." Through narrowed lids, Sari studied her. For all she knew, Marianne, the little maid with candid cornflower blue eyes and dimples, the artless giggle and eagerness for her friendship, was play acting.

"Out." Sari jerked her head at the door.

"No." Moving to a chair, the English girl seated herself, folding her hands and leaning back with an air that said she had as much or even more right as Sari to be here. She was not about to be shooed away. "Will you give me a minute? I beg you, Sari."

"Why should I? You made a fool of me. You led me on to prattle about my love for castles. You pretended you didn't know how to reach the battlements. You didn't tell the truth about the top floor because you knew there are four illegal aliens up there."

"Wrong." Emphatically, Marianne shook her head. "I admit I'd had my suspicions that there was something fishy going on, but how could I have known anything? When you told me about the circular staircase, I tried it out for myself, and then I realized what is going on. And I was appalled."

Sari eyed her with mistrust. After seeing and hearing her with Monty, how could she believe anything Marianne said? More than once she had seen that clear-eyed mask drop long enough to give a glimpse of the emotions Marianne kept under wraps. If Ron had been masquerading, why not also this harmless-appearing girl. The slow minutes passed as they faced off.

Finally, Marianne cleared her throat and in a firm voice said, "Sari, believe whatever you want, but I haven't lied to you. There is something I've wanted to tell you, though. When your grandmother brought us all together on Monday evening, it sounded as if she might be planning to deed over Hudspith Castle to you. Everyone heard it, and I believe you've been in peril ever since you arrived. How else can you account for all the scary things that have been happening?"

Sari stared at the maid as her words slowly registered. This marvelous, fairy-tale castle would be hers—the vaulted great hall with its sparkling chandelier, the priceless trestle table and high-backed chairs in the dining salon, the graceful, majestic staircase one usually sees only in one's dreams.

"Well, if someone is worried I'll accept anything, much less this place, from my grandmother, he's crazy. I don't want this castle or anything else that belongs to her."

"She loves you."

"Loves me? That's a laugh. No, she never has, and as for myself, I surely don't love her." Before she was aware of what was about to happen, all the pent-up resentment broke through the dam to hit Sari with the force of a tidal wave. A surge of emotion swept over her and left her floundering, disoriented and giddy in its wake.

Through the eddying mists came Marianne's halting whisper, "Why? Why are you so bitter? What the Duchess may have done to cause such loathing is not the issue. You claim to know and love God. You know what the Bible says about unconditional love and forgiveness. She needs yours. Can't you find any room in your heart for her?"

"Listen." Sari shook her finger at the maid. "Your grand Duchess is to blame for everything bad that's ever happened to me. Because of her selfishness, my parents barely eked out a living on the mission field. She never wrote a letter, not one, even when my dad was dying. As far as she was concerned, I never existed. I was a kid, alone, and she didn't care. And you expect me to love her?"

"Begging your pardon, but does that give you the right to hate her? Knowing the Word as you do, you know it doesn't. Oh, Sari, I'm so thankful for the Bible verse that tells us that if we come to God and confess our sins, He always forgives. I can't help suggesting that maybe you ought to—" Marianne's words dissolved into choking sobs as she jumped up and fled through the sitting room.

What nerve, Sari told herself. I don't need Marianne to tell me what I should do. She shrugged angrily as her eyes made contact with an object on the bedside table. She blinked. A Bible? This was a strange thing to find in her grandmother's room.

Do tell! She is like a lot of other people, Sari thought. She keeps this here for the sake of appearances. It was a lovely Bible and Sari could not resist picking it up even as she sneered aloud, "She certainly doesn't read this."

Guilt stung her. How long had her own Bible lain unopened. Gathering dust.

When she saw the name on the dedication page, she laughed at her mistake. "I should have known. Of course this doesn't belong to her; it's Ollie's."

It was one of the large new study editions and very beautiful. How her father would have appreciated a Bible like this, with supple leather covers unmarred by scratches, and fine smooth sheets. His Bible had been all dog-eared with the pages falling out because he could never afford to purchase a new one.

Sari's mind was full of memory pictures as she

thumbed through his favorite Old Testament books, the ones where he had never failed to find encouragement and the firm assurance of God's love and care.

Suddenly, she gasped. It was not because of a snapshot of her grandmother, which she found between the fortieth and forty-first chapters of Isaiah, but because right beside it, next to the spine of the Book, there was something of much greater interest.

It was a long, paper thin, silver key.

Sari's scalp prickled. What a strange place in which to keep it. That thought was followed by another: what if this is the answer?

Did she dare hope this was the key that would, literally, unlock the mystery of the Duchess' disappearance? Or would that be too bizarre a coincidence?

After a moment's contemplation, Sari decided she would not question why a key was in a Bible. The need to find the Duchess was all that mattered. Therefore, she would go on the hopeful assumption that it really was the key that would open the door to her grandmother's secret refuge.

Before long, her newly-found enthusiasm had evaporated and she stood back and scanned the room. She had searched every square inch, every chink and fissure of wall and floor, had tapped for hollow spaces, but without success. There would be no point in going over it again. There was no matching keyhole in this room. But she couldn't give up. She had to find it, so she would keep on searching.

Sari was exhausted, but time was of the essence and she knew she had come to the end of that legendary rope people talk about. Her intuition was fair, her hunches so-so, her evaluation nearly always adequate. For what loomed as a monumental task, however, she needed help. Supernatural help.

She argued with herself. How could she ask God to do anything for her when she was so unworthy? Did she even have the right to claim the promise of the Scripture verse Marianne had quoted? As scalding tears squeezed between her lashes, Sari reached out blindly and fell on her knees beside the bed.

"I don't need to tell you how I've messed up my life," she admitted in a hushed voice, "and that it's all because I didn't stay close to you. I'm going to take you at your word and cast myself on your mercy. Are you ready, God? Will you please forgive me? I haven't been letting my light shine for you, but everything will be different from now on." After a moment she added wryly, "That's a ridiculous thing to say because you and I both know I'm likely to fail. But with you helping me, I promise to keep trying."

It was a simple prayer, but it left Sari feeling relieved as the weight of emotional baggage she had been carrying for years was lifted off. As she bowed before God, her heart was filled with gratitude and it seemed so natural to humbly lay before Him her search for the Duchess and to praise Him for the answer she felt sure He would give.

A few moments later she opened her eyes with the strong impression that the key really had not been placed by random in this Bible and in this particular section. She felt impelled to read, starting at the top of the left-hand page and on through to the bottom of the one facing. She was looking for a clue of some kind, but if there was one to be found, she was slow in catching on.

How she wanted to believe there was a message hidden between the lines. How maddening to find it eluding her in every verse. All Sari could perceive were the majestic, inspired words of the prophet Isaiah.

Wriggling her stiff shoulder blades, she breathed a desperate request: "Oh, dear Lord, I don't know what I'm looking for. Please help me." She stopped in her tracks. That verse, the final one in Chapter 40; it rang a bell.

She prayed again, asking for insight and understanding. Then she read aloud: "Those who hope in the Lord will renew their strength. They will soar on wings like eagles; they will run and not grow weary, they will walk and not be faint."

Eagles. The word fairly jumped off the page. According to Monty and Jessica, the Duchess had a "penchant for eagles" and the golden eagle on the Hudspith Crest was her "pride and joy." Was it just grasping for straws to assume the entrance to her refuge was behind the eagle on the mantel in the great hall?

Sari hurried toward the door, but then forced herself to stop and think. Isaiah's eagles tied in with the one above the fireplace, but what about the snapshot that had been nestling next to the key?

Turning, Sari ran back for it, wishing that somehow it could talk.

In a way, it did.

It was an ordinary shot of her grandmother seated beside the chess table in the gazebo and, at first glance, there did not seem to be anything unusual about the picture until Sari's gaze zeroed in on the object in the Duchess' hand.

That was not a chessman she was holding. It was long and shiny, and Sari knew exactly how the prophet Daniel must have felt when he successfully deciphered the writing on the wall of King Belshazzar's palace.

Chapter Eighteen

With the key and snapshot clutched in her hand, Sari was out of the suite in a flash, streaking through the hushed corridors, when she saw a shadow emerging from the gloom.

Smothering a scream, she sprang back. Then she saw who it was. Had she not been so excited, she would have been terrified of this man with burning coals for eyes.

"Monty!"

"If it isn't our resident night owl. Are you on an errand?"

"Ah, does it really matter?"

"I'd say so; yes. Have you looked at the time? It's getting on toward morning, and I find you coming out of the Duchess' rooms. Be a good lass and tell me what you're up to."

In her nervousness Sari dropped the key, which landed with a soft clink on the polished floor. She quickly recovered it, the sharp silver edges cutting into her palm as she tightened her fist around the key.

"Truth is, I believe she's right here in the castle, and I hoped to come across something that might help me find her."

"Dear, I don't blame you for fretting about her. I would worry too, if this were the first time she has dropped out of circulation for a bit. Even though I believe she is all right, I'm always eager to know she's safe when this happens."

Sari was bewildered by her uncle. She had seen the other side of the coin and had heard enough to make her wary, yet he seemed so sincere. "Of course I'd like to believe you, Monty."

"Then there is no problem, is there?" he said in an ingratiating manner. "So, if you'll kindly give me that key you're holding, I'll take it from here."

"No." With hands behind her back, Sari shook her head.

"Look, young lady, time's wasting, so don't be daft. Hand it over." His brows drew together in a heavy frown. "Come on now, or you'll be in deep trouble."

It definitely was the wrong thing for Monty to say. It brought vividly back to mind the scene in the great hall and the fear that had gripped Sari then.

"You're threatening me, aren't you, but I'm not giving it to you. You can't have the key. It stays with me!"

His response came with an abruptness that took away her breath: his smile vanished and he shifted his position. And he came too close.

Later, when Sari thought of what happened next, all she saw was a blur. And it rolled in slow motion. She watched as Monty lunged for her, clutching her arm while her right leg was going back in the proper karate stance and her left knee was bending. She was raising her right knee now and her foot was striking in a side-thrust kick with her heel aimed at his solar plexus. As it connected he crashed with a thud against a heavy highboy, slid down its length and passed out.

Sari hung her head, drew a deep breath and thought, Michael would have been proud of me. Reluctant pupil though I was, when it came down to the nitty-gritty and faced with this husky enemy, I guess what I learned was more than enough. Thank you, Michael.

"Have a nice nap," she told the recumbent Monty, as she quickly resumed her flight. Passing the mantel in the great hall, she barely glanced at the bejeweled coat of arms. This eagle certainly was top drawer, but it was his cousin masquerading as a weather vane haughtily riding the breeze above the gazebo that drew her like a beacon through the opalescent paleness of dawn, across the garden straight toward the summerhouse.

Winded and pressing against a crick in her side, Sari fell onto a bench. The enclosure was overpoweringly sweet with the scent of roses. She sniffed with appreciation. Gauging its width and thickness, she held the key before her. Then, turning her attention to the marble-squared playing board, she ran her fingers from side to side over the satiny surface. Again and again, searching for an infinitesimal opening made to accommodate the extremely delicate key.

When her temples began to throb and her back ached from leaning over the table, she rested against the cushions. Then the thought of Monty regaining consciousness and following her across the garden made her wipe the nervous perspiration off her hands and get back to work. In that second she saw it. It really was there, a slit between two of the black and white squares.

In the next instant, it had disappeared, but she kept her eyes fastened on the spot. When the breeze ruffled the ramblers and the shadows shifted, she pounced. Her steady fingers inserted the key. The octagonal table on its broad pedestal rolled to one side to expose a descending flight of steps and she quickly started down.

At the bottom, Sari groped until she found a light switch. She went along a passageway that burrowed under the castle's east wing until it ended in front of a teakwood door. Was this it? Was this her grandmother's hideaway? And when they came face to face at last, would she answer all of Sari's questions?

Eagerly, Sari knocked. She wasn't sure she heard anything and knocked again. Then she heard a faint answering voice.

"Yes?"

The doorknob turned easily under her hand and, with her heart in her mouth, Sari stepped in. She found herself in a room that was much like a very large storm cellar. But there the resemblance ended.

With silken hangings, Oriental scatter rugs, and low lighting, the scene before her could have been lifted from The Thousand and One Nights, with color accents running the spectrum through greens and lavender to sunshine yellow. All of which, Sari suspected, had been selected to complement the personal coloring of the woman who reclined on a low divan.

She was dressed for the part in an exotic, diaphanous robe and shod in slippers covered with glass beads. Though time had exacted its toll and her Titian tresses were fading to a dusky rose-gray, she was still the comely lady whose likeness graced the magic door leading to the third floor tower. The Duchess.

The woman had been caught off guard. With a gasp her head came up sharply.

"Who are you? What do you want?" Trembling, the Duchess pulled herself up to a sitting position. The bracelets on her arms tinkled as she leaned forward and extended a hand. "Come over here so I can see you."

"Please don't be alarmed. I'm not going to hurt you." Sari was weak with relief. She had actually located her grandmother.

With a wary eye on the bullterriers, Sari moved nearer. Then she relaxed. Winston and Churchill really were toy dogs, nothing more than porcelain-like sculptures that breathed. Pedicured, shampooed and brushed, these canines were harmless. All they would be good for was a quiet chuckle.

Afraid that her sudden appearance had been too much of a shock for the Duchess, Sari asked, "Are you all right?"

"To be honest, it gave me a jolt to see that door open. And I'm not very happy to realize a perfect stranger knows about this room. I've never told anyone about it. Who are you?" Suddenly the Duchess' eyes widened as she stared. "But, why of course, with that red hair I would know you anywhere. You're Sari, aren't you?"

"Yes, I'm Sari." The Duchess seemed to be making an effort to steady her breathing as she motioned toward an ottoman.

"Why don't you sit where I can look at you? Please." Her face crumpled as tears filled her eyes.

"Words can't express how glad I am to see you. If I'd been in your shoes and received a summons from someone who had never acknowledged me, I'm afraid I would have turned a deaf ear. Oh, of course I would." Her lips trembled. "My child, what a fool, what a colossal fool I've been."

Sari turned away so her grandmother wouldn't see how she pitied her. Oh yes, there was no mistake about it: she had acted the fool, but she was to be pitied. The quaver in her voice betrayed the reason she had filled her life with hustle-bustle, travel, a bulging portfolio, and rare antiques. Even the fanciful ambiance of this novel setup that included, of all things, a round bed and a life-sized carousel Arabian horse with a flowing mane and flashing agate eyes.

Nothing could ever blot out the terrible estrangement from her own flesh and blood that had turned the Duchess into a restless, lonely woman.

Sympathy filled Sari's heart as she reached out to God on behalf of the errant grandparent for whom she had sworn never to pray. Tears burned behind her lids but before she could think of anything to say, her grandmother reached for a silver bowl.

"Would you care for some grapes?" The Duchess smiled engagingly but a shiver of apprehension shot through Sari as she detected a tremor in the hand holding the bowl.

"Here in Arizona we have some fine fruit, but back home in Northumberland, where I grew up—and the flowers. They were gorgeous! When I married Geoff, we decorated with the Hudspith Centennial Rose." The softly-lined face suddenly lost its animation, the aquamarine eyes their sparkle. After a pause, the Duchess continued on what to her granddaughter sounded like a forcedly-cheerful note.

"I was so naïve, I actually believed that with that marriage all my problems would somehow miraculously dissolve into thin air, but I had not figured on the extenuating circumstances. Oh, extenuating circumstances! I came to hate those words."

Listening to the low murmur, Sari had become clinical once more. The file folder that bore the Duchess' name was open. Like other women who had sat uneasily beside her desk, hyperventilating and prattling irrelevancies, her grandmother was inventing aimless small talk. *She isn't well. It's her health, just as Oscar feared. She probably can't sleep. That's why she is sitting up in the middle of the night.*

"Are you sure you feel all right?" Sari asked. With a graceful lift of shoulders, the Duchess shrugged off Sari's concern and patted her hand.

"I'm fine, and we must talk. Do some catching up."

"Yes, it's long overdue." Sari's remark had slipped out. To cover it, she added, "I've been here since Tuesday afternoon, but of course you didn't know that. Everybody has been worried because you didn't show up. Even your attorney, Mr. Drayton, was concerned."

"Oscar?"

"Yes. He's been here the entire time. Actually, he's the one who finally figured if you had a secret hideaway, that's where you might be. He was afraid you had become ill, so we decided I should try to locate you."

"Dear Oscar. People usually take my vagaries in stride so I didn't think twice about staying down here these few days until your arrival." Her face clouded again. "I had my reasons, but I'm sorry for being such a bother."

"People care about you. I'm just glad I found you."

"I don't see how you can say that." The Duchess shook her head. "What reason have I ever given you to care if I live or die?"

"Shh." Sari leaned over and held her grandmother's wrist. "This is too much for you." The pulse beneath Sari's fingers was racing. "I think we should wait until later today to visit."

"How can I wait? There is so much I want to know. For instance, I am curious about how you found my little sanctuary."

"It was the snapshot in the Bible in your bedroom that gave it away—and the key," Sari admitted. "I've always been interested in castles, so I started to look for a secret passageway. I hated to invade your privacy but until I searched your rooms and found the key and the picture, I had no clue where such a passageway could be."

"Ah, yes. Practically on his deathbed, my beloved hubby made what he called his 'peace with God' and began studying the Word. In fact, he wore out one Bible. I was very jealous of the time he spent reading what I thought was 'poppycock,' but it made Ollie happy. He and I loved eagles, and you can imagine how fond he was of the verse in Isaiah that speaks about them. After he died, I could think of no more appropriate spot for Ollie's special key than right there in the new Bible I had bought for him." The Duchess' expression softened. "I can't believe you are really here. And now, tell me all about yourself."

Now that the moment was here, Sari was asking herself if she really did want to bring it all out in the open: the heartache, the corroding, vindictive hatred that had cost her sleepless nights and so many tears.

She had sought and found forgiveness in the process of laying on the altar the less-than-charitable attitudes that had dominated her. Now did she want to rehash the past? What if the old venom should spring up again from the roots that had twined so tightly around her very soul?

"What I have to say can wait. I'd rather listen to you. If you feel like it," Sari suggested.

"Oh, I do. I'm all wound up and I need to talk. I really want you to know everything, especially about where I am, today, at this moment. The best word to describe it is 'stupendous' and, being your father's daughter, I am sure you would agree." She was speaking in riddles.

"I'm afraid I don't follow you."

"You will. But I need to start with Friday."

"When you went to L.A.?"

"Yes. I want to tell you about last Friday. About my doctor's appointment and what happened afterwards."

Chapter Nineteen

It had begun like any other smoggy late August day in the City of the Angels, the Duchess said. Her close friend Aileen, an elderly widow like herself, picked her up at her hotel after breakfast.

They headed for the mall for some shopping, then drove to the Medical Center for the Duchess' appointment. To while away the time until her internist was ready for her, the Duchess picked up a magazine, turned the pages, then tossed it aside with a groan.

"Aileen, to tell the truth, I've been more than a bit wary about this visit," she nervously admitted. "I can't help wondering why Dr. Brad had me go through that battery of tests again. What did he expect to find?"

"Oh, come on now." Aileen patted her hand encouragingly. "You know you've never looked better, and I don't think you have a thing to worry about. He'll give you a clean bill of health, then we'll celebrate at the Regal Biltmore. It will be a lovely evening. They say that new comedian is great, and we can catch his show after we eat. Won't that be fun?"

Before the Duchess could answer, a nurse beckoned and she followed her into the examining room to be weighed. She was escorted into the office where her doctor waited behind a glass-topped desk. A smile creased his pleasant face as he stood to shake her hand.

"It's good, as always, to see you. How are you, my dear?"

"I feel fine. I really do!" The Duchess screwed up her face. "That's what all your patients say, isn't it? But please don't keep me in suspense. Do you have the results of my lab work?"

"Yes, and I've gone over them thoroughly. You're aware that for some time now we have been closely monitoring these glands of yours. And you know that I believe it is only fair to be as straightforward as possible. So I have to tell you that your condition has worsened considerably."

"Oh." Her heart seemed to stop. Dr. Brad is such a dear, she thought. He doesn't talk down to me as though I were senile, and this is probably worse for him than it is for me. Swallowing hard she said, "I appreciate your honesty, Doctor."

"You don't know how sorry I am." He came around the desk and held her hands as he said kindly, "I wish I could offer some guarantees as far as time is concerned, and I certainly won't be offended if you'd like to get a second opinion."

"That isn't necessary. You've looked after me for many years and I trust you implicitly. You've been right on the money about everything else, so why not this?"

Even though she put on an outward show of cheerfulness as she walked back to the waiting room, the Duchess couldn't hide the fact that she was stunned and a bit shaky. Aileen took one look at her face and put a steadying arm about her.

"You look washed out. Don't tell me. Was it bad?"

"Very bad. He said—" The Duchess gulped and pulled her friend toward the door. "Aileen, let's get out of here." As the two women rode the elevator to the parking basement, the Duchess repeated Dr. Brad's words.

"He says I'm not getting better, only worse. And he can't tell me how long I've got left. If I hadn't been going to Dr. Brad for years and if I didn't have the utmost confidence in him I'd do what he suggested and get another opinion. But I do trust him."

"Oh, I'm so sorry. And I know how you feel," the Duchess' friend said. "You stuck by me last year when I had to undergo all those horrid chemotherapy treatments, remember? I want you to know that now, whatever you have to do, I'll be there with you. But listen," Aileen said, "just wait and see. You'll prove Dr. Brad wrong yet. I know you will!"

"No, I feel it in my old bones." The Duchess sighed. "He spoke the truth." In the car, she made an effort to cast off her dark mood. "We had some fun today, didn't we? I lost count of how many dresses we tried on. It's pretty ironic, you know. I've made it through three quarters of a century, I'm the perpetual flitterer, and I have my thumb in any number of interesting pies." Her mouth turned down at the corners. "I actually believed I'd live to see the year two thousand and beyond."

"You will, you will! And I'll repeat what you said to me awhile back: you can't give up. You are too vital, too alive, and this is not the end of the world."

"I hear what you're saying, Aileen. No, I can't retreat from life just because I've learned I can count on only X-number of months. Or weeks."

The Duchess was glad her friend had made reservations for an early dinner. The evening promised to take her mind off the distressing verdict. But when they were seated in the elegant hotel dining room and she opened automatically to the wine page in the menu, she groaned.

"Dr. Brad said this is a no-no. How am I going to exist without my cocktails?"

When their food was served, she looked at the baked

salmon and pushed away her plate. "My appetite has flown."

"I understand. Shall we leave?"

"But you haven't finished your dinner, Aileen. And there's that fabulous entertainer." The Duchess' silver-haired companion gathered up her purse and gloves and signaled for the check.

"That's not what's important. You are. So we'll get some doggy bags."

When they reached the Duchess' hotel, Aileen insisted on going with her to her suite.

"You've had quite a shock. What you need is some hot tea. Isn't that what you Britishers always say? I'll plug in the electric kettle."

The Duchess liked this comfortable old residential hotel in a quiet neighborhood. The baroque decor made her feel at home because it reminded her of her castle near Prescott. On this evening, though, the dark paneling and heavy drapes seemed too symbolic of the way her life would be from now on, circumspect and slowed down to a crawl. It made her want to scream. While they waited for the water to boil, Aileen picked up the newspaper.

"I can't believe the television listings tonight," she complained. "There's practically nothing on except those tiresome political debates." She flipped the dial on the set. "See? Boring, boring." She was about to switch it off when the Duchess leaned forward.

"Wait. You just passed something. Go back. There, that's it! That must be the big religious meeting they've been talking about."

"I guess it is. The stadium looks packed."

"Maybe, after what Dr. Brad told me, I ought to be thinking about the hereafter. My hereafter." The Duchess reached for her jacket. "I'm going over there. Do you want to come?"

"What? You aren't serious? You are serious. Well, all

right. I can't let you go by yourself. But are you sure it won't make you feel morbid?"

"Who knows? I can't feel any worse than I do already."

In a few moments they were outside under the marquee and the doorman was whistling for a cab. A taxi appeared in seconds and the driver hopped out to help the doorman tuck them into the rear seat.

"And where can I take you ladies?" he asked. He raised his eyebrows at their reply.

"Well sure, everybody knows where the stadium is. But I hear there's standing room only." He shrugged, "As for me, I don't have any use for such things. It seems to have become part of our culture, though, so I guess everybody owes it to themselves to go at least once just to say they've been."

Traffic was light and they made good time, but the evangelist had already opened his Bible and begun to speak before they found an empty space near the top row. The women panted as they fell into the metal seats.

In the unfamiliar setting, the Duchess squirmed, resisting the urge to look around to see if anyone she knew was in the audience. She wondered if Aileen felt as out of place as she did, though it really didn't matter. It would be over soon. And she settled back.

There was something so disturbingly familiar in the text being quoted that, to her surprise, the Duchess suddenly found herself hanging on the words, listening with her mind and her heart. After a moment she recalled that Ollie had spoken those very words on his death bed: I am the resurrection and the life. He who believes in me will live, even though he dies; and whoever lives and believes in me will never die.

The speaker's finger seemed to be pointing straight at her and the Duchess shivered with the realization that she was poised on the brink of eternity and was not prepared to meet God. She squeezed her eyes closed, but she was unable to tune out the sound of the deep voice urging people to leave their seats.

"Come down to the front. I'll be waiting for you, and I'd like to pray for you, so won't you come? I don't know what your burden is, but God does, and He cares. Have you lost hope? He can give you hope. Would you like to know real peace? He can give you peace that is so perfect that no one has ever been able to describe it. So don't wait a moment longer. Come to Him right now." Through her wet lashes, the Duchess glanced at Aileen.

"You'll probably think I'm completely daft but I want to do it. Will you go with me?"

"I was going to ask you the same thing." Her friend's lips trembled.

Arm in arm, they made their way to ground level and across the field to join the crowd standing in front of the platform. A few moments later, as she repeated the words of a simple prayer of repentance, the Duchess, oblivious to the tears that were ruining her mascara, could feel the Lord taking her proud, soiled heart and lovingly wiping it clean. At that very moment God had poured into her empty being a warm, comforting presence. She knew nothing would ever be the same again.

Though she had intended to fly back to Arizona on Saturday morning, nothing could have pulled the Duchess away from the remaining days of the campaign, so she stayed on. She and Aileen purchased Bibles for themselves, then spent hours studying them. They felt just like natives in a jungle outpost who had heard for the first time in their lives the good news of God's redeeming love.

And that afternoon she called the law firm in Phoenix. "Hello, Oscar. Have I caught you in a mellow mood?" she asked. "I'm aware it's the weekend, but I'd really appreciate your being a dear and doing a big favor for me." Oscar Drayton, wondering why the old lady wanted to get in touch with her son at this late date, promised to contact the Mission Board in London.

"I'll get right on it now," he assured her.

While the Duchess waited for her attorney to return her call, she told Aileen for the first time about her son and the absence of communication between them.

"I was so wrong for so many years. Oh, Aileen, I want Sam to rejoice with me that I've found the Lord. God has forgiven my sins, and I want Sam to forgive me, too. I long to rebuild the bridge between us, but what if Sam won't meet me halfway?"

"My dear, Sam is a man of God. You have to believe he'll understand and be willing to let bygones be bygones." Praying, the Duchess huddled beside the telephone and grabbed it on the first ring.

"Oscar! Did you get through to London?" The Duchess paled. "Oh dear, oh dear."

She was awash in self-loathing, remorse and the need to atone. Now she knew she had waited too long. It was forever too late. The voice brought her to her senses. "Yes," she said in a choked voice, "I'm still here. Would you please repeat that, Oscar?"

Aileen sat quietly while the Duchess listened, pressed her brow as though smoothing away painful memories, then issued some orders and hung up.

"So what was that all about?" Aileen inquired.

Reaching for a tissue and drying her eyes, the Duchess groaned, "He says my son passed away several years ago. Now I'll never be able to make things right."

After a moment she drew a shaky breath and managed a lopsided smile. "But hear this, Aileen. He told me I have a grandchild. Sam's girl. Can you believe it, Aileen? I have a granddaughter. And Oscar is going to find her for me."

The Duchess looked at Aileen with glistening eyes. "I've just learned I am living on borrowed time, but that doesn't seem so important any longer. What matters is that I am not afraid to die. I've never been able to say that before. I found God. No, I got that backward. He found me! And He has turned my life around."

The Duchess was humbly aware that a merciful God was showing her a new direction and giving her a new goal. So in spite of her doctor's prognosis, she felt very hopeful and excited as she arrived back at Hudspith Castle on Monday evening and called her staff together.

"I've decided to do something worthwhile with this old castle," she announced, "something to show that I've been here when it's my time to leave this earth. I've come home with some wonderful plans, some innovations that I'm hoping will induce my granddaughter to help me launch the project I have in mind."

She waited for their reaction and the astonishment generated by her pronouncement was so profound that she couldn't help but laugh.

"Believe me," she told them, "I am just as surprised as all of you to find that I do have a grandchild. She is a young lady and my attorney has discovered that she lives in New York City. He is asking her to fly to Arizona and she will be here on Friday."

Springing the news on her people was the easy part, but the Duchess cringed when she thought of meeting the stranger who represented nothing less than an unmerited chance to turn back the calendar. She sadly reminded herself that maybe it might be only wishful thinking that Sari would want to see her. Why should she?

After a restless night the Duchess awoke on Tuesday, feeling blue and discouraged until she remembered that she was not alone. Even if the worst were to happen and Sari refused to have anything to do with her—she could hardly blame her for that—the Duchess would never be alone again. Not when the Creator of heaven and earth had promised to be with her always.

Trying to recall how it went, she began humming one of the songs she had heard at the campaign, pulled herself out of bed and received a nasty shock. While she slept, someone had been rummaging in her wall safe.

"Oh my," she murmured, "who would take my will?" But then, her pang of dismay was more sentimental than anything else, "And Ollie's little map is gone!"

Chapter Twenty

Though it was just a rough pencil-sketched diagram, the precious map Ollie had made for the Duchess was a priceless reminder of her husband. Whenever she looked at it, the years would fall away. It would seem like only yesterday that they had sat on the bank of Castle Pond and Ollie, dark eyes gleaming with the excitement of a true inventor, shared his plans for a little mountain railroad.

She could still hear him chuckling as he said, "I've got the route all laid out in my head, and I think this is something you'll go for. My darling, you told me the surveyor's map of this property is on file in Prescott, but you never could understand it. Well, just so you'll know where our railroad will be, I'm going to draw you a map that will make sense to you."

The Duchess had watched curiously as Ollie, leaning back against the broad trunk of a pine, quickly drafted an outline of the castle and its environs, then smiled fondly at her. "I know my ideas usually sound to you like so much Greek. All these wiggly lines delineating contours, and X's and O's indicating landmarks. But here goes."

Her eyes widened with appreciation as he added his own unique touches: a toadstool here, a bird's nest there, and stepping stones across the tiny river on the other side of the pond.

As Ollie ran his fingers down her cheek and tousled her hair, she wondered again what she'd ever do without this jovial Welshman who used to moonlight as an engineer on one of those real Great Little Trains of Wales.

"Do you remember the day we met?" she asked. She never tired of talking about it. She had gone over to the sleepy resort town of Tywyn to take care of business and saw Ollie sitting in the hotel lobby. He had looked as if he didn't have a friend in the world.

"How can a guy ever forget the luckiest day of his life?" he said as he hugged her. "Love, I still recall every word you said to me. You noticed my engineer's cap and asked how I liked working on the Talyllyn. I was a goner, sweetheart, from the first second I looked into your beautiful eyes and thought they were the color of Cardigan Bay at twilight."

Ollie added in his lilting musical voice, "You really knew how to flatter a fellow. Like asking me to tell you all about Wales's historic narrow gauge steam railways." He grinned, "I couldn't believe a successful business lady like yourself didn't know anything about them."

"I really didn't. But I learned a lot from you that day."

"You know, as a kid growing up in Llangollen I knew that the 'Little Trains' had been used for transporting local people and their produce and slate from the North Wales slate quarries." Ollie got a faraway look in his eyes. "It's inevitable that they'd grow into a tourist attraction that would give a tremendous boost to the local economy, but never in my wildest dreams did I imagine I'd be an engineer on one of them. Sweetheart, you made me proud to be connected with something that is helping to preserve my Welsh heritage." Her husband kissed her hand. "I do love you for it."

When time ran out for him, the crude map was the Duchess' only reminder of Oliver's desire to build for her his version of a Welsh mountain railroad. Thus it had become a treasured keepsake.

And now the map was gone.

Baffled, the Duchess stood in front of the safe. Who could have rifled it? Nothing like this had ever happened, though it was common knowledge around the castle that she never locked her safe, just as she did not bar the door to her suite. Why should she do so, when everyone here was her trusted friend?

Nevertheless, talking about "innovations" and a hitherto unknown granddaughter must have prompted somebody to creep into her room and walk away with her will. And Ollie's map. Apparently someone wished to study them. But why?

By the time she climbed into her white slacks, pink blouse frothy with lace at neckline and wrists, and white boots and sauntered downstairs, the Duchess was able to take a charitable posture toward the only person who would have any reason to take anything out of the wall safe.

Of course she had no proof, and she felt disloyal to even entertain the suspicion that it could be Monty, but of all the faces looking up at her last night as she shared the news of Sari's imminent arrival, it had been his strong tanned one that mirrored the greatest alarm.

The Duchess had composed herself before she reached the terrace where he was lingering over his coffee and the Prescott *Courier*. When he jumped up to hold her chair, she was able to give him a smile.

"Good morning, Monty dear. Isn't it a pretty day?"

As she buttered her toast, she was agonizingly aware of his clouded brown eyes on her and her heart sank. That's just the way he looked last night, she thought.

Didn't Monty know that no matter what came of her meeting with Sari, he had a special place in her world and her life and that Hudspith Castle would always be his home?

As soon as she could, the Duchess finished her breakfast and, with her dogs, headed for the lovely summerhouse Ollie had created for her. She believed there was something therapeutic to be derived from working with growing things. But this morning as the Duchess trimmed the roses, she could not put Monty out of her thoughts. Was he worried she'd do something foolish? That sweet boy loves this place as much as I do, she reminded herself. He must know I'd never do anything out of the way without consulting him and that certainly includes modifying my will.

"The will is one thing, but why," she wondered aloud, "should Monty want to study Ollie's funny little map? He knows all there is to know about this castle." She caught her breath. "Well, almost everything."

She sighed, wishing Ollie were here with her. Of all people, he would know how she should handle the dilemma she was facing. As always, he'd be able to tell her what to do.

Her hands had been shaky on the garden shears and her head ached. The Duchess felt guilty for distrusting Monty, and she regretted being so cowardly that she couldn't come right out and ask him why he had gone into her safe like a thief in the night.

Suddenly she had felt extremely tired and for a dizzy moment the gazebo threatened to spin around. It steadied as she clutched the edge of the chess table and tried to pray, but she could find no comfort. She was so new at this business of trusting and the words were slow in forming.

The counselor at the stadium had recommended spending time in meditation and prayer as the best way to prepare oneself to deal with problems. The Duchess was sure the emotions she was feeling toward her adopted son constituted a problem, one with which at this stressful moment she felt totally incapable of handling.

She needed to think. The tempting thought of getting away by herself came to mind. This was what she and Ollie had often done. They would close the door on their immediate surroundings and retreat. This seemed to be what was called for now: to take time to figure, with God's help, what her next step should be.

It was at this instant that the Duchess decided to drop out of sight—literally—until the weekend when her lawyer and Sari would be on the scene. After all, Jessica was very capable of making preparations for Sari's arrival, so what was to stop her? And she knew it was exactly what Ollie would have suggested.

Chapter Twenty-one

After the Duchess stopped speaking, silence filled her hideaway. Then Sari gave a deep sigh.

"Ohhh. What a rare person your Ollie was. No wonder you love this room where you spent precious times together."

The touch of her grandmother's hand on hers brought tears to Sari's eyes. This feeling of togetherness, of comfort and caring was what she had missed all her life. She wanted to hang onto it.

"But how can I accept your doctor's verdict?" Sari cried. "Not when I just found you. How can we lose each other now?"

"My child, God is in control. And that's a miracle! After I had ignored God—and I mean totally ignored Him—He received me as His own child. I felt whole. The only thing missing was my reunion with your father. I knew that was not to happen when Oscar told me he had passed away."

Sari thought that someday she might tell her about her father's last days and his poor funeral, but not now. She said only, "What a horrible shock that must have been."

"I was destroyed. What could I do now about the miserable parent-child relationship that was rooted in the dim past of what might have been? If only my husband Geoffrey had been able to love Sam. If only affairs had not come to a head on the eve of Sam's leaving for Cambridge." The Duchess sighed heavily.

"I think this is too much for you. We've talked enough. You should rest," Sari said.

"No, please let me go on. I must go on. It's just that I'm so ashamed. Oh, the recollection of that terrible night in the London house when my son asked me point-blank about his father! That memory still makes me shudder." She shuddered now.

Sari protested, "You don't have to go into it, you know. Wait awhile."

"But I want to tell you how it was. Sari dear, let me, as we say in England, put you in the picture. While I talk, do you think you can just sort of shut out everything around us—this room and all and see what happened?"

"I'll try," Sari told her. "I'll do my best. I'll try to see."

Sam, who was usually so punctual, had been late for supper in the Mayfair house that night, the Duchess told Sari. When he failed to show up, she had given orders to the kitchen help to put the meal in the warming oven. For two hours she sat nursing her cocktail and wondered what was keeping him.

Her son had been acting nervous and on edge lately, and she was glad he would have a couple weeks of relaxation before he went to the university. She finally heard his steps in the entry and the butler's greeting. She breathed easier. When Sam came into the drawing room, she held up her face for his kiss.

Without a word he brushed past her to begin drumming his fingers on the mantel. The curve of his chin looked stiff and his broad brow was creased. The cozy drawing room with its comfortable sofas and velvet footstools suddenly felt cold.

"Cook made your favorite kidney pie. You mustn't hurt her feelings," the Duchess hinted. "Will you wash up quickly, so we can sit down?"

"Sorry; I seem to have lost my appetite during the last fortnight. I'm not hungry."

"Sammy, what are you talking about?"

In a quick change of subject he jerked around, pointed a finger at her and thundered, "Don't you agree you owe me the truth? I say it's high time you opened the closet door and let out the skeletons."

"The what?" The Duchess was sure she had misunderstood.

"The skeletons. The secrets. There never was any love lost between my father and me. After all, what chance did I ever have to get to know him? And that was good, wasn't it, because that meant I'd never find out he was crazy. Why didn't you tell me he was sick, sick in the head?"

The Duchess had been struck dumb. As she looked up at him he added, "Why wasn't I told he had been committed to an asylum, or wasn't I entitled to be privy to that kind of juicy information? Do you have any idea how it felt to learn it from a stranger?"

"Darling, you were away at Gordonstoun, and then you went off to tour the Continent. I didn't think you should be burdened with the knowledge. That's why I didn't tell you," the Duchess stammered.

"You should have been decent enough to tell me!" His response shook the room as he tapped his temple and bellowed, "I've done a lot of checking. Some authorities claim the tendency to insanity is transmitted through the genes and sick people are prone to do themselves in. Among other things. Why didn't you come clean? Why didn't you tell me about my father?"

"Oh, dear son. You're afraid you've inherited a mental weakness. My child, you are in no danger of going off the spool." She took a steadying gulp of air and admitted to him what she had never revealed to another living soul. "Sam, Geoffrey wasn't your birth father."

She brushed aside his snort of incredulity. "No, of course you can't take it in; not just yet. But I am telling you the truth. I was married to Geoffrey's cousin for three years. I guess the fact that our marriage was a secret lent a sort of romantic aura to it. I loved the bonny Scottish lochs and the crags enshrouded in fog, the moors carpeted with heather, and our small thatched cottage." Her mouth twisted as she sadly added, "I should have known the bliss couldn't last." With arms folded, her outraged son stared implacably at her bowed head while she sobbed into a handkerchief.

"There was a terrible collision when the car Andy was driving went out of control," she groaned. "As I stood by his casket I would have been satisfied to curl up and die, too. But by then, I knew I was going to have something—a dear little somebody to go on living for. My baby. You, Sammy."

The Duchess' admission did not elicit a sympathetic response. On the contrary, the drawing room seemed to vibrate with her son's scorn, and she was impaled on his icy glance.

"What a jolly good story. But it sure didn't take you long to bounce back, did it? Geoffrey, the fellow I always thought was my father, was conveniently waiting in the wings. And you snapped up the bloke."

"You make it sound so tawdry. The truth is, he had traced me to that isolated hamlet in Northern Scotland. When he suddenly appeared on my doorstep and proposed to me, I accepted. He had loved me ever since we were all children together, and he was willing to help me get my life together. Sam, he gave me the strength I needed to carry on. So, when he asked that I promise never to tell anyone—or my child—that I had been his cousin's wife and that Andrew was your father, well, I gave him my word."

"I don't believe this! How could you agree to such an immoral request?" Sam clenched his fists. His neck throbbed; his face flushed.

"I am so terribly sorry." His mother hung her head. "At the time, it struck me as very endearing that Geoffrey cared enough to want to be known as my baby's papa and that we'd be a family. Can't you see that I did what I thought would be best for you? And do you understand you need never be concerned about Geoffrey's mental disintegration? It's no threat to you."

"What's wrong with you, anyway? Don't you see how wicked it was to deny me the truth about my paternity? It's the ultimate betrayal! I vow I'll never, never forgive you."

To her horror, Sam flung himself in a rage from the house, stopping at the bottom of the steps only long enough to wheel and pull a case from his pocket.

"You can have my bloody keys!" he shouted. "I won't be needing them, because I'll never be coming back."

Chapter Twenty-two

———————⬬———————

Now as the Duchess swallowed painfully and fell back against her cushions, the very air of her hideaway seemed to throb with regret. Sitting at her grandmother's feet, Sari had been able to feel the emotion that, like an electric current, had crackled between mother and son in that Mayfair drawing room when Sam, the victim of her lies, realized how grossly he had been cheated. Sari knew exactly how he had felt, because the Duchess had cheated her, too.

"I wished with all my being that I could have mustered the courage to tell Sam everything," the Duchess whispered. Her hands were clenching and unclenching in her lap. "But how could I tell my son about the black, jealous moods into which Geoffrey withdrew following my baby's entrance into the world? Sam was such a sweet miniature of Andrew. Even as a newborn, he had the same intelligent forehead and patrician nose that was a constant, abrasive reminder of the cousin Geoffrey had always resented."

Although she thought she already knew the answer, Sari asked softly, "Did you think your husband might hurt the baby?"

"Exactly. He displayed homicidal tendencies with such alarming frequency that I finally did something that broke my heart: I sent Sammy away where he'd be safe. There was no other path open to me. I knew that blessed child wondered why he couldn't stay at home like other boys, but how could I explain?

"That final night when the truth about his parentage came out I just couldn't confess the brutal beatings I had endured, or Geoffrey's inordinate resentment of even the basic, ordinary attentions I paid my child—like changing his nappies. I could have told your father about Geoffrey's threats to broadcast to the world the truth behind Andrew's fatal accident if I should step out of line. But I was simply not at all sure Sam could have handled it."

Sari suddenly realized that she had been holding her breath. Her grandmother was not the only one here who was "wound up." For Sari, these moments of disclosure possessed a healing quality. But even while some of the vexing puzzles—such as those evoked by the documents Sari had found in the Duchess' safe—were being solved, new ones popped up. Such as this latest, Andrew's "fatal accident." The Duchess made it sound so significant. Why? Could this be one of the "extenuating circumstances" she had bemoaned?

Wincing, the older woman spread her hands. "I was so bereft when Sam left me without the solace of even a solitary picture of him to keep the memories green. Geoffrey had forbidden me to have any pictures taken. He smashed my camera so I wouldn't be able to take any myself. I was forced to obey his cruel edict. I knuckled under to a tyrant. Oh, why couldn't I stand up to him?"

"Because you were a tiny ant, and he was a giant foot determined to squash you."

"I never thought of it that way." The Duchess gave a shaky laugh. A pang of worry darted into Sari's mind. How fragile her grandmother was.

"Haven't we talked long enough?"

"There's just a bit more. I really did mean it when I told your father I was sorry. I wrote faithfully to him while he was at Cambridge. Sent checks for his expenses and pocket money. He acknowledged neither letters nor checks, so when he telephoned just before he sailed for India, I was in no frame of mind to hear he had 'found the Lord' and was on his way to serve as a missionary. A missionary. What an affront!"

Tears traced down her cheeks as she wailed, "After passing me by for six long years, this arrogant lad thought he could wipe out his neglect with a belated 'I love you, Mum' and I suddenly had enough. I closed my heart to him. Oh, Sari, I really did. I paid him back with good measure. It was my turn now and, worldling that I was, all I cared about was my pride. I ordered my secretary to rip into shreds—without opening—any envelope that might arrive with the Wyatt name in the corner."

"So that's why you never answered when I wrote to you," Sari said sadly. "You never even read my letter telling you Daddy was dying."

"Oh, dear child. Now you know what a vile person I have been. All I can say is that I would give everything I own to go back and do it all over again and do it right." Straightening up, the Duchess tried on a brave smile that crinkled the little crow's-feet by her eyes. "The Holy Spirit has so graciously ministered to me during these days. He has helped me to stop being apprehensive, and I'm going to trust Him to give me the strength to live in victory from now on."

With bracelets tinkling, she made a wide gesture. "So what do you think of my home away from home?" She pointed out her compact kitchen. "See the microwave and blender and the teensy refrigerator-freezer. Over there is my stereo system, and beyond that folding door is a dear little rose-tiled bathroom."

While Sari wagged her head in awe, the Duchess added, "Aren't you dying to ask if that carousel horse works? He really does. In fact, he bucks and jumps and twists and gives you a great workout. I just know that when Michael gets here, he'll love it."

"What? Did you say Michael?" The pain that stabbed Sari's heart made her gasp. "Do you mean Michael Hancock? And he is coming here to Arizona?"

"Yes. Oscar's New York search team turned him up almost immediately and on Monday, before I left the coast, he called me at the hotel. Now there's a young man who is so in love that it just made me feel warm all over to listen to him. Oh yes, make no mistake, you are very special to Michael, and he has been counting the days until you can be together again."

"After the way I treated him?" If only it were true. "I didn't even tell him face to face I was breaking our engagement. I sent his beautiful ring back by messenger!" Sari remembered his soft kisses falling on her brow, her cheek, her lips and sadly shook her head. "How could he still love me?"

"I guess you'll just have to take my word for it until you see him in about ten hours or so. Anyway, we had this nice chat, and I learned so much about you, dear, and how you felt about me." The Duchess grimaced. "It was not flattering, but what could I expect?"

"What could Michael tell you? I never said anything to him."

"You didn't have to. He is an extremely astute fellow. He had been aware for a long time how burdened you were, but he cared enough for you to pray for you and let you work it out for yourself. When the detectives told him why they were looking for you, he recalled a remark you had let drop the day you got my telegram. That was when Michael realized that I was the underlying reason for your unhappy state. Frankly, after our conversation, I wasn't at all sure I would see you. And, of course, it seemed almost too much to hope that you could feel anything but utter disdain for me."

As Sari remembered how she felt the first evening she spent here in the castle, she was forced to admit her grandmother had made a painful point. It was only a short time ago when she had held Ollie's Bible and cried out to God that her attitude toward her grandmother had softened.

Thoughtfully, Sari considered the Duchess and weighed the pros and cons of telling her all that had been going on in her absence: Oscar's "accident" and Ron's near-fatal plunge from the balcony. The "whispering stones" that led Sari to the Mexican guests in the tower. And what if Sari aired her suspicions where Monty was concerned? Should she tell the Duchess he had been trying to make her run away?

This grandmother of hers did not bear even the faintest resemblance to the formidable foe Sari had anticipated. She was an elderly woman who had found God in the twilight of her life. And she had only a small share of time left. It might be best to shelve the bad news.

"I was taking a lot for granted, banking on your willingness to collaborate with me on the plans I have been working on." The Duchess' brows raised in a wry frown. "But the plain truth is, they won't even get off the ground without you."

Sari could not have imagined what she was about to hear when her grandmother lowered her voice and theatrically announced, "I aim to transform the castle into a home for missionaries, I mean, a comfortable place where God's valiant servants can rest and recoup their energies when they come home on leave. Does that sound wonderful, or what?"

"It certainly does." Sari wasn't sure she understood her grandmother's words. "Did you say a 'home for missionaries'?"

"Yes. I want it to be an oasis of peace and tranquillity

minus any stress, so they'll be able to regain some equilibrium after the hardships of the mission field. In other words, a quiet spot where physical and spiritual batteries can be recharged."

"You should see your eyes sparkle as you talk about this fantastic plan."

"That's because I believe the Lord put it into my mind. Of course, I don't have the wrinkles completely worked out," the Duchess admitted, "but that's something we can do together, if you want to. And would you like us to dedicate it to the memory of your dear father and mother?" The Duchess had to stop because Sari was hugging her and they were both crying. After a moment, the older woman dried her cheeks and continued.

"There'll be plenty of R and R. Things like horseback riding, nature trails and get this—a kids' farm, a kind of petting zoo, where they can help take care of the animals. And what do you think? Shouldn't we have a couple of those fuzzy little llamas?"

The Duchess was so eager to share all her goodies with God's family that she sounded as thrilled as any Aladdin with a magic lamp in her hands.

"I don't want to die before I've done this one thing for God. All I'm asking from Him is time, just a little time."

As a tear slid off the Duchess' nose, Sari cried, "Grandma, no! I won't let you talk that way." And she heard herself saying words that sounded so new and so right: "I love you, Grandma." She knew it was true and that the last, lingering vestiges of hate and ill-will were gone.

When the Duchess spoke again, Sari had to lean forward to hear. "I need to tell you something else. Ollie begged me to get in touch with your father. But I had a very good reason for not doing so. You see, child, the estrangement kept him from ever knowing the truth."

Like a hungry fish lured toward the bait, Sari's senses leaped. Finally. This was it. The rest of the story.

But, apparently, she was not going to hear it. Not yet.

Chapter Twenty-three

Suddenly the teakwood door slammed like a thunderbolt. But the Duchess' expression of alarm melted immediately into one of genuine pleasure. "Jessica!"

"Yes, it's me. Thought I'd join the party," Jessica drawled. "I know you are wondering how I got in. Well, I was looking out an upstairs window when I saw Sari running into the gazebo. Then she didn't wait to figure how to close that clever trap door, so here I am." She glanced about. "This is really cute. And to think you've kept it a deep dark secret from the rest of us."

"How long have you been standing out there, dear?"

"Long enough to hear everything. I'm sorry, but I'm afraid you are going to have to revise your big plans because I cannot allow you to go through with them. It's obvious now that you have a granddaughter that you'll revise your will and in the long run the castle will belong to Sari. And don't you see, that can never be."

As she stared at the Duchess' daughter-in-law, Sari was unable to believe the words she was hearing, or the sarcastic tone of Jessica's voice. She looked different, too. Leaning nonchalantly against a large crystal jardinière with her hands stuck in her belt, her smug manner sent out danger signals. What was wrong with Jessica?

"Dear, I am sure you realize you do not have a thing to say about this," the Duchess reminded her.

"Is that so? Well, Monty does. He—" Jessica spun about as her husband's baritone filled the room.

"What on earth is this place? Mum, it seems I didn't know you as well as I thought. And I'm incredibly relieved. You've had us all at sixes and sevens." Monty kissed the Duchess and dropped a sheet of paper into her lap. "Your will. And I believe this is your property as well." And he handed her Ollie's map.

"Ohhh!" With tears running down her face, the Duchess beamed at him. "Dear Monty. I don't know why you took these, but thank you for bringing them back. Especially this precious map."

"I didn't take it. I found it in Jessica's desk with this. Look—" A faded document crinkled when he smoothed it on the Duchess' knee. "This is a map, too, but if you compare it with Ollie's handiwork, it's—no offense—a bit more like the genuine article. It even has little bits of dried mud adhering to it. I think my wife had better start explaining."

"That map belonged to my dad," Jessica answered tersely. "After the Duchess told us she had some new plans for the castle, I was just comparing the two. And who can blame me for being curious about her will? Monty, keep out of something that doesn't concern you."

"I beg to differ. It is very much my concern," Monty said. "Mother, if you fit this map over Ollie's, the perimeters line up and other measurements as well. See where the castle is? Now read the words right there. Aren't they enough to quicken the blood flowing in any prospector's veins?"

The Duchess' words were faint. "I don't understand. It says 'Gold Mine.' Monty, we aren't—are we sitting on a gold mine?"

"According to this, yes. Do you recall Jessica telling us that after her father was killed in a cave-in, she came across a map in his things that showed he had found gold? It seemed he had put off filing a claim and somebody else went in and built on that particular section of land. Jessica didn't say where it was, but when I found these two maps together in her desk, a lot of things suddenly made sense. I now know that she never believed it was too late to do anything about her father's discovery."

"That's right, I didn't think it was too late!" His wife's scream was ugly. "It's never too late!"

"Sure," he replied coldly, "and that's why you deliberately set your cap for me, isn't it? You never loved me. You figured marrying me would be the way to get your hands on the gold." Pulling at his mustache, and with beetling brows, Monty's dark eyes bored into her.

"I can read you like a book, Jess. I know how vulnerable you've felt since Sari showed up on Tuesday. I didn't know what you might do to frighten her away, or to actually hurt her. Ironic, isn't it, that Ron was the one who connected with the balcony railing outside her room? Marianne has been worried to death, and I've been running in circles trying to keep a watchful eye on Sari. Shielding her from you! Jess, don't you find that rather sad? I admit I do."

His wife's evident surprise was no greater than Sari's as she realized that Monty's provocative behavior from the very beginning had been for her protection. This meant that on the night of her arrival at the castle he had been the one who checked her bedroom door to make sure she'd locked it. But was Monty telling the truth? How could she believe the word of someone who was mixed up in the importation and dissemination of illegal immigrants?

"What you just said is pure nonsense," Sari blurted. "Jessica's been so sweet to me. She wouldn't harm me.

Jessica, tell him it isn't so."

"Why should I deny it? Do you honestly believe I ought to have jumped for joy when the Duchess announced she had a granddaughter? So what, if Monty's only an adopted son. The fortune under this eyesore on the Arizona landscape belongs to him. To us! And no Sari-come-lately will stand in the way."

Feeling sick, Sari stammered, "You know, your father may have stumbled across only a tiny strain of gold. If there really is any beneath the castle, you'd have to find out by— Oh no, Jessica, you wouldn't!"

"I would," she hissed. "I'd raze it tomorrow, level it to the ground, and nobody will stop me. If that's what it takes to get my dad's gold, so be it. See this little nugget on my locket? Well, there's a whole lot more where this came from and I'm going to get it."

"No, dear," the Duchess reproved her. "We are not going to let that happen. Jessica, it's only natural you would feel the way you do about your father's precious treasure, if indeed he did find one. But that's history. What is done, is done, so forget the gold, child."

"I can't forget it. I won't!"

Monty turned to the Duchess. "For awhile now I've had a gut feeling that something was going on here, and half an hour ago I learned what it is. Mother, there is more than a gold mine at stake. Thanks to the traveling that so often takes you and me away from home, my wife has found herself a lucrative hobby. Lucrative and illicit. Naturally she doesn't work alone. One of her partners is her cousin: Ron Cooper."

"Jessica," Monty grimly suggested as he turned to her, "why don't you tell all about your people-moving activities and call it by its rightful name: smuggling aliens across our southern border. Tell how you have been using the third floor tower of this isolated castle as your base of operations. You may as well talk, since Oscar spilled it all, a few moments ago."

"Oscar?" Jessica spat the name. "He's lying!"

"On Wednesday he asked you to meet him in one of the bunkhouses. He had found out what you were doing and implored you to get out of the racket. He warned you he was going to the police, and that's when you went at him with a knife. Because of his extra padding, it missed a vital spot by a hair, thank God."

"I don't believe he told you any such thing. Why would he spin a tall tale like that?"

"It was the truth. Oscar has many contacts on both sides of the border. He is trusted by all and people tell him things." Suddenly, Monty lost his composure. "Jess, you sure are a piece of work. What came over you? Why would you get involved in something so corrupt?"

"Monty, please," the Duchess interrupted. "I insist on knowing what is going on. People-moving. Smuggling of aliens. Are you talking about Mexicans and that Jessica and Ron and others have been bringing them into this country and selling them?"

Sari empathized with the Duchess' attempt to grasp the full import of this ugly disclosure. Sari had been somewhat prepared for it. The real shocker, though, was Jessica's involvement. Sari was overwhelmed with relief that Monty and Marianne had nothing to do with it.

"Mother, they are a link in a chain. The organization, according to Drayton, has contacts, suppliers and buyers in several states. Their method is to bypass the normal immigration process, for a fee, naturally. It's like the 'Underground Railroad' of American history, and Hudspith Castle is one of the stations."

Monty riveted his eyes on his wife. "But this railroad does not lead to freedom, does it? And this isn't a 'safe house.' No, it's anything but. Explain about the four Mexican girls you are keeping on ice in the tower, even as we speak."

"How can such a thing be possible? Illegal aliens

hidden here in *my* home." Outrage vibrated in the Duchess' protest. "The very idea is ludicrous!"

"And think what it would do to your peerless reputation if the news leaked out," her daughter-in-law suggested sardonically. "Of course, you could sweep it under the rug as you did that other time. I mean, how your money averted a nasty scandal years ago. You probably forget that in a weak moment you cried on Oscar's shoulder and told him all about your first husband's addiction that caused a wreck and a Scotsman and his family were wiped out. The whole clan, Duchess, including five children."

"Oscar would never have violated our lawyer-client confidentiality," the Duchess whispered.

"Oh, he never talked to me about this. It was just one of those things. I was sitting in the library and you didn't give me a chance to get out. I heard how you and your husband's cousin Geoffrey bought the silence of all the witnesses, so no one would know that Andrew was so stoned he wouldn't have known the difference between the gas pedal and the brake. He was guilty of vehicular homicide, wasn't he, Duchess? He should have gone to jail for a long time, maybe for life. You cared about your family's good name then, and I'll bet you still do. You really don't want to risk a scandal now, do you?"

In an instant, Sari was on her knees beside the divan, her hands over her grandmother's icy cold ones. Jessica had just supplied the missing piece of the puzzle.

"You were shielding Daddy all along, weren't you? You didn't want him to ever have to live with the shame. You loved him, Grandma," she said softly, "you really did love him."

"Don't think you're going to stop me," Jessica screamed. "The gold is mine and I'm going to have it!" She pointed a shaking finger at Sari, "You're to blame. Why did you ever come to Arizona?"

She moved so swiftly that Sari nearly missed the

change in her expression as Jessica pulled a long pair of kitchen shears from her pocket and started forward. But Sari recognized the raw hate in her eyes. After all, she had lived with her own raw hate for so long. But she couldn't move out of Jessica's way. She felt as though she had been turned to stone.

The bullterriers, however, could read Jessica's intent. In what Sari would describe later as two streaks of greased lightning, they moved to stop Jessica in midstride.

They did not touch her, just lifted off and came down very close to her, their heads cocked and their sleek muscles quivering as though daring her to come on. Instead, Jessica took a hasty step backward, stumbled, and banged into the bulky cut glass jardinière.

It was over quickly. Though Monty dashed toward her, he could not prevent his wife from lurching onto spiky shards as the huge vase splintered beneath her. Sari felt herself fainting and turned her gaze away from the sight, but she could not shut out the sound of Jessica's dying gasp.

That was the last thing Sari knew until she raised her eyelids and found herself stretched out on her grandmother's round bed and realized, with a suffocating surge of gratitude, that she was still alive. Because two toy dogs with protective instincts and hearts of gold had come to her defense, she was here with her grandmother and she was safe.

And in a few hours she would see Michael.

Epilogue

The beautiful, winding staircase in Hudspith Castle just seemed to have been designed for weddings. The great hall was filled with flowers and guests as Sari, decked in her grandmother's own billowing lace gown with the embroidered pearl-encrusted train sweeping behind her, came drifting down on Monty's arm.

In the midst of her joy she felt a wave of sadness as she thought of her parents. If only they could have been here to share this happy day with her.

Sari could picture her mother, elegant in a shimmering sari, her glossy black hair caught up in her heirloom comb. She would have tears of joy in her eyes. And her father—he would have escorted her proudly into the great hall to "give her away" to Michael. This would be Mother and Daddy's day.

At the entrance into the hall, Sari saw the Duchess, whose face was filled with love for Sari and gratitude to God for His bountiful blessings. She knew her grandmother felt deep satisfaction in knowing she had been able to help Him work a few miracles.

The fact that Ron Cooper was seated beside the Duchess and Oscar Drayton was just one of those miracles. At the Duchess' request, Oscar had contacted the INS on Ron's behalf and talked with the Investigation unit. Ron had freely admitted his involvement in the transporting of illegal aliens and his decision to quit. In a meeting in the U.S. Attorney's office Ron had volunteered to give all the information he possessed regarding such activity and was granted full and complete immunity from prosecution.

And clustered at the kitchen door to watch the wedding was another miracle: Marita, Teresa, Berta, and Rosa with her sister Lupe. They all were so thrilled with their green cards and their jobs right here in the castle.

As Sari had expected, the Duchess had taken the girls' plight to heart. She had wasted no time or money starting the wheels turning to find Lupe. Her tears had mingled with Rosa's when they heard the news that her sister had been found unharmed in a seedy San Francisco bar. She and Rosa had flown to the coast to bring Lupe home.

"If you want to stay in this country, I'll be your sponsor," she told the girls. "The castle can be your home." She had confessed to Sari, "I consider these precious Mexican girls my own personal 'mission field.'"

By the light of the myriad twinkles from the chandelier, Sari met her groom beneath an archway covered with roses from the summerhouse. She handed her bouquet to her dimpled maid of honor, but Sari doubted Marianne saw anyone but Monty, whose diamond solitaire sparkled on her finger.

Michael's eloquent eyes spoke of his affection for Sari. Before they turned to face the minister, he whispered, "I love you, precious, now and forever and ever and ever."

The Duchess wept as she proclaimed it the sweetest wedding she had ever seen.

As the months passed into years, Sari's grandmother benefited from the advances of modern medical research. The Duchess called several arrests of her particular type cancer "heavenly reprieves," which indeed they were, granting time for all of her ambitious plans to take shape just as she had envisioned them.

Because she opened up her heart and home and everything in it, the Castle Hudspith truly became the answer to a tired missionary's dream. On Thursday afternoons the ladies met to sip tea from her delicate Spode cups. Because, as their hostess told them, an English castle is synonymous with "high tea," and you don't drink English tea from a mug.

For the missionary men there was something more appropriate: a short nine-hole golf course that spread over the castle grounds. Plus a roomful of clubs. And carts. Michael, senior pastor of a large church in Prescott, often made up a foursome while Sari and Grandma, along with her ever-present companions Winston and Churchill, rode on Ollie's miniature railway to watch them tee off.

Unashamedly sentimental, the Duchess had enthusiastically taken over the project Ollie had roughed out to make the Great Little Train a reality. It was a quaint memorial to their love. The jumbo, life-size plaster board cutout of an engineer, the smiling, friendly Welshman named Ollie with his hand on the throttle, looked just as he had so many years ago on the Tywyn run.

In the years since Sari's "command appearance," Hudspith Castle had evolved into a peaceful oasis in the southwestern desert. Children loved this happy haven. Especially Sari's and Marianne's. For them, it was the best of all worlds where there were always new and interesting playmates, missionary children who would never forget the months they spent in an enchanted castle with singing stones.

Since the castle's transformation, the only kind of whispers one could hear were those of youngsters running up and down the circular staircase that led to the parapet-enclosed playroom crowning Sari's tower.

Everyone at the castle believed that the Duke of Rhysbury would agree with what they had going in their wonderful fairy-tale castle and that it was worth infinitely more than any treasure that might have been buried in the earth beneath it.

Because all of them had so much love to share with each other and the missionaries God sent their way, why wouldn't Ollie be happy to know they were still sitting on a gold mine?

About the Author

Sally Hawthorne had always dreamed of being a missionary. That dream came true when she and her husband, Jack, sailed to South America in 1942. It was wartime. They traveled in convoy. The ship ahead of them and the one behind them were both sunk by enemy submarines.

Seventeen years in the high Andes of Bolivia were followed by assignments in New York City, the Southwest, and Costa Rica. In order to minister in these cultures, the Hawthornes learned the Inca language, Quechua, and Spanish.

Ten years ago, Sally and Jack collaborated on a Hawthorne Family History in celebration of their Golden Wedding Anniversary. The Lord has blessed them with five children, a dozen grandchildren, and eight great-grandchildren.

Sally believes a Christian writer can be a force for God in the world and considers it a high calling to be a scribe for Him. Besides *Whispering Stones*, she has written about Bolivia in *Cloud Country Sojourn* and a novel *All My Tomorrows* with its locale in Spain.

Sally enjoys speaking to women's groups, sometimes with the help of a colorful visual aid.

For Speaking Requests Please Contact
LANGMARC SPEAKERS BUREAU
P.O. 33817
San Antonio, Texas 78265-3817
1-800-864-1648

TO ORDER YOUR COPY
Whispering Stones

If unavailable at your favorite bookstore, LangMarc Publishing will fill your order within 24 hours.
✉ Postal orders: LangMarc Publishing • P.O. 33817 • San Antonio, Texas 78265-3817

U.S.A. cost: $12.95 + $2 postage
($3.00 for priority mail)
Canada: $15.95 + $4 postage

☎ or call 1-800-864-1648
Fax: 210-822-5014

Bookstores: LangMarc books are available from Spring Arbor, Ingram, Baker and Taylor

Please send payment with order:
_____   Books at $12.95   _____
            Sales tax (Texas only)7.75%   _____
            Shipping   _____
            Check enclosed   _____

— — — — — — — — — — — — — — — — — — — —

Send _____ copy of *Whispering Stones* to:

_____

_____

_____

Phone: _____

Check enclosed: _____